A TIME TRAVEL ADVENTURE

S. J. SMOLIGA

THIS BOOK IS FICTIONAL AND ANY RELATIONSHIP TO NAMES, DATES, INCIDENTS, SITUATIONS, PRODUCTS OR PLACES ARE PURELY COINCIDENTAL.

ANY MENTION TO HISTORICAL NAMES, DATES, INCIDENTS, SITUATIONS, PRODUCTS OR PLACES ARE FROM SOURCES ASSUMED RELIABLE BY THE AUTHOR AND ARE FOR ENTERTAINMENT PURPOSES ONLY. THE ACCURACY OF THE HISTORICAL CONTENT IS NOT GUARANTEED.

THE TIME SURVEYOR

BOOK 1 - THE BEGINNING

ISBN # 0-9729354-0-1

PUBLISHED IN THE UNITED STATES OF AMERICA BY:

SIDONA SYSTEMS INC.

WEST LINN, OREGON 97068-0402

EMAIL: thetimesurveyor@netzero.com

FIRST EDITION [E1] 6" X 9": MAY, 2003

1 – 04132003 – 1 – 500 + R

This book is dedicated to my wife Donna and my daughter Jennifer who edited and provided suggestions for this book.

CHAPTER 1

Time travel had always been on Chris Manlee's mind. As a young boy he had watched his father experimenting in the basement of their home. Not with actual time travel, but developing a method or device to accomplish it. His father's time traveling device was never functional – mainly because the parts needed weren't available in the '70s. Chris didn't start developing his own mode of time travel until the late 1990s, when he quit his job (he made a lot of money in the stock market in the late 1990s) and was able to spend full time on it. He never told Jennifer, his wife, that his interest in time travel started when he was a young boy – guess he didn't think it was important, even though they both spent many years developing their time traveling machine. They referred to it as the time surveyor and called it the 'TS' – not for any particular reason, but sort of a code that only they and anyone they wanted to tell would know it by this alias. Chris and Jennifer lived on an acreage he inherited with his brother after his parents died. Chris eventually bought his brother's share. This gave them the privacy to develop the TS. They kept the development secret, except for Chris's brother Rich and his family (Donna his wife and their son John). Chris and his brother had always been close.

The story begins on August 7, 2004, Rich and Chris are in the TS building (Chris built especially for the TS) and were talking about the time traveling machine. Rich asked Chris how long he had been working on the time traveling machine. It was about five years since he started developing it. He had some problems in the design of the power unit with the laser capacitors, but with Jennifer's help he had almost solved that problem. Jennifer's education, a doctorial degree in physics with emphasis in lasers, sure helped with the power unit design.

Rich had confidence in his brother's ability and asked where his first time travel destination would be. Chris wanted to visit their parents in 1971 and have their father store the plans for his time traveling device in a safe place – "so he could retrieve it in the future" should anything happen to their father. Chris was 'extremely annoyed' (actually he used some stronger language) with their aunt and uncle who had gone to the house after their parents died in 1972 and basically destroyed all the papers and notes their father had written. This was probably the main reason they didn't go to see their aunt and uncle. Rich did come to their defense in saying that they probably didn't realize what they were throwing out and with the age he and Chris were probably couldn't explain it to them. Chris told his brother that when he was growing up, he would sometimes 'daydream' of time travel, but didn't tell anyone. Their conversations once again turned to traveling to see their parents in '71.

"Our parents would be younger than us. How'd we tell them who we are?" asked Chris.

"Don't know – good question – we probably could come up with something."

"Is Jennifer enthused about the time traveling machine?" Rich asked.

Almost with perfect timing, she walked in with Donna and her son. Jennifer heard the question and hesitatingly commented that she liked the idea of time travel but was concerned that it was untested and anything could go wrong. She was concerned about its travel worthiness. If there were problems they could end up in a time they didn't want.

Chris buffered her comments a bit by saying that she was very important to the project by her experience with lasers and that he could not have developed it this far without her help.

Donna was probably more enthused with it and expressed that it would be 'fantastic' to see the future and how civilization had advanced.

Rich asked him what his confidence level was for the TS to operate properly. Very positive, Chris said that it should work without any major problems. The tests he had done so far turned out to be very promising. He probably would have it ready for testing in a short while. Rich asked him what he based his time travel theory on.

"Well, for future travel the best I could explain it would be like this. Imagine you are in a boat in a river and anchored in the middle. Upstream there's a block of wood. The choice you have is to break anchor, start the motor on your boat and drive upstream to the wood, or you could leave the boat anchored and get a rope, lasso the wood and pull it to you. If the current floated it to you then it would be like normal time."

"How'd it apply to time travel?" asked Donna.

"Imagine the TS as the boat in the river and the time you want to go to is the piece of wood. What the TS does is stay in the same place and pull the time to it."

"How would it work for the past?" questioned Rich.

Chris went on to explain that the block of wood would have to be down stream. "You would have to rope it and pull it against the current."

Jennifer supported Chris's concept that it should work in theory but the only way to find out is to try it. That could actually be in the next few weeks if everything went well.

John, Donna and Rich's son was sitting in the TS. Being a small boy he was amazed at the different equipment especially the time dials. The keys weren't in the TS so there was no chance of John going on a time travel.

It was getting late and Rich and his family had a long drive back to California the next day. Rich went over to the TS and got John. They never did really explain to John what the TS was, except that it was a 'special car'. They all walked to the house after Chris had locked the TS and the TS building.

The next morning, after breakfast, Chris and Rich carried the suitcases to the car. Rich looked over to the front door of the house. Donna, Jennifer and young John were walking towards them.

"Everything in the car?" asked Donna.

"Yep, all set to go."

They gave the traditional hugs and handshakes. Donna opened the back door and John got in. She buckled him in and closed the door.

Rich got in the driver's seat and Donna walked around the car to the passenger's side. Rich rolled down the window and asked Chris to keep him informed of his progress.

Donna crouched down just so she could see through Rich's window and said, "come and visit with us anytime. Why not get together at Christmas like we used to, we have plenty of room."

Jennifer walked up to Rich's window. "Will think about it and let you know."

"Well, better get on the road." Rich started the car and drove away.

All of them got along very well and Jennifer expressed that she was going to miss them.

"We probably should plan to go there for Christmas this year," Chris said.

"Yes, we haven't been on a vacation in about five years."

The reason for no vacation was simple - they had been working on the TS. Jennifer hadn't even been to visit her parents in Florida since they moved there.

Slowly they walked to the house.

"Want some coffee?"

"Yes, thanks!"

She got two mugs from the cupboard and set one in front of Chris and one where she was going to sit then poured the coffee.

"Are you going to work on the TS today?"

"Yes, after I finish my coffee, I'll go and check the power supply and control modules. What are you going to do?"

"I've got some house cleaning to do, change the beds and do the laundry."

He asked if he could help her with anything, but Jennifer knew that he was anxious to get back working in the TS. He picked up his coffee, got up and walked to the front door.

"If you need any help with anything just holler. I'll be in the TS building."

He walked out to the TS building, looked into the TS – pleased with the progress they had made. He sat in front of the computers and began to work.

CHAPTER 2

The Manlee's built the TS into a late model SUV. Many types of vehicles had been considered but the SUV seemed the most appropriate. It was a standard unit with no 'frills'. In the back area was the laser, capacitors and the control modules to be out of the way so both front and back seats could be used. He painted on the hood in small letters 'TS – THE TIME SURVEYOR' for no reason, but probably to distinguish it as his and Jennifer's accomplishment. One piece of equipment that he added to the unit was a GPS (Global Positioning System) and a tracking system so he could find out the location of the TS if it was moved after a time trip. He eventually wanted to put in a system so he could dial the coordinates and time travel there from his 'home' spot. This was low on his list at present – he wanted to get the TS working properly first.

Inside the TS, two inches from the dash, he mounted on a stand, three time indicators. These indicators were rectangular in shape, about 3/4 of an inch by 7 inches and located in a vertical row. The display numbers were black with a light orange background.

Each indicator had its own special purpose. The top indicator was the present date and time. The one in the middle was the time of destination and the bottom one the travel rate. Each indicator had 14 positions with the numbers separated by thumbwheels. The first 6 positions displayed the year (The display was for a maximum of 999,999 years in the future or past) the next 2 for the month, the next 2 were for the day. The last 4 were for the time (0 to 2400 hours). Gauges indicating the amount of energy remaining and the outside temperature were also on the dash. There was a small red light to indicate a malfunction with the unit and space for an additional push button for aborting the time travel.

He hadn't installed the 'abort' push button because the calculation on how to abort the time travel was complex. An aborted time travel could result in entering an unscheduled time era if it was not integrated into the system properly. Therefore, once the time travel was initiated it couldn't be stopped – the TS had to travel to the predetermined time destination.

To initiate the time travel, he installed a toggle switch with a 3 inch handle on the dash to the left of the steering wheel. Moving it up initiated the time travel.

The main hardware – control and power modules were installed. The area he had yet to complete was the software for the control modules monitoring the boost and normal energy. He had spent many hours trying to get the module to control the boost energy accurately and many times had come very close, but because of a software and sometimes a hardware bug, it was not satisfactory. He was getting close, and after some final adjustments, his persistence paid off when, today, it worked to within an extremely close tolerance. This would give good accuracy upon arriving at the destination – probably within a few minutes on a short destination and a few hours on the maximum distance traveled. The energy discharge rate was very critical. If it was not controlled accurately, the TS could overshoot the arrival time by hours and as much as days on a long time travel.

On August 15, 2004 in the afternoon, he began the simulation tests. After a few hours, most of the tests were within his estimated tolerances. The TS was ready for the first time travel.

It was about 5:30 in the evening when he went to the house to tell Jennifer about his plan to travel to 1971 and see his parents. She knew this time would come and deep down her 'bit of fear' was realized. She was in the kitchen cooking dinner when Chris came into the room and told her. She was puzzled that he wanted to go to 1971 – why would he want to see his parents that had died in 1972.

He explained that he wanted to get the plans his father had produced for a time travel device he was developing in the early '70s. Not because he didn't have trust in the TS, but his father's design was much smaller. He went on to explain how he would watch his father develop the time traveling device, and how his interest in time travel evolved. What happened to the design and any documents he had, she questioned? Chris explained that they were thrown out by his aunt and uncle after his parents died.

He told her that there was never a working model, but remembered his father making sketches and in some cases putting a description on the drawing of what the part should do.

"I'd like to go back and retrieve his plans or at least get my father to put them in a safe place so I can retrieve them in the future."

She questioned him - why hadn't he told her about his father's time traveling device before? He didn't think it was important to mention and really didn't think of telling her until now.

Overall, she was actually happy that the tests had gone well, but still wanted him to do some further test to determine if it was safe. If something went wrong one could get lost in some time period, not being able to get back. Chris assured her that all would go well, although he really didn't know for sure. He told her that the control module software for the energy transfer worked well today. Under simulation it supplied energy at a very precise rate.

Jennifer, still being cautious, suggested that he build a miniature one, something with just a few hours time trip into the future. He thought for a minute and reluctantly agreed - it was probably a good idea. It wouldn't take long to build one. He could use a model of an SUV that he saw in one of the hobby stores in the city.

Tomorrow he would get the model and build a miniature TS. Jennifer smiled her approval.

After dinner they relaxed with Chris watching some TV and Jennifer reading her physics journal. Around 10:30 pm he turned the TV off, told her he was tired and was going to bed. Jennifer said she would be along soon but wanted to finish reading an article in the journal.

CHAPTER 3

August 16, 2004. It was after 8:00 in the morning. Chris didn't sleep well - he was anxious to get started on the time traveling model. He hurried through breakfast and did the calculations on the size of the model he would need – at least two feet long. It was noon before he was done. Jennifer was in the house getting some lunch ready when Chris yelled to her that he was going to pick up the model.

"Do you want some lunch?"

"No thanks, just wanted to let you know I'm going to pick up the model."

The drive to the store didn't take long. He had walked by it many times, and like a kid he would look in the window at the models. Some had amazing design detail. Most of them were radio-controlled units 2 or 3 feet long for serious miniature drag racing. Others were just for 'playing around' in the dirt.

He walked to a corner display and read the description on the box.

- FULL REMOTE CONTROL WITH MINATURE TV MONITOR FOR VIEWING THE "ROAD".
- REMOTE START
- REMOTE STOP
- CONTROLLABLE UP TO 2500 FEET.
- REMOVABLE ROOF FOR EASY ACCESS INTO THE MODEL.
- THIRTY INCHES LONG.

.... PLUS OTHER FEATURES.

It had all the features he wanted. This one would do what he needed and was a decent price.

Chris was still looking at the model when a store clerk walked up behind him.

"Can I help you?"

Chris turned around a little startled. "Yes."

The clerk was a man in his early thirties dressed in faded blue jeans with a black and white checkered shirt. He started his sales pitch by explaining that it was a fine model and came in just 'a while ago'. Some of the enhanced features he showed Chris included a miniature engine, not as fully functional as the real one, but it worked very well.

"Looks great, I'd like this one," Chris said.

"Good choice, what are you going to use it for?"

Chris didn't tell him the truth, but reluctantly said he was going to use it just for fun and run it on his property. The clerk went to the back to get one in a box. A few minutes later he returned and set the long narrow box on the counter. Puffing slightly he 'rang' it up on the cash register.

The clerk asked if it was cash, check or credit card.

Chris took out his wallet and handed him a credit card. The clerk ran the card through the machine.

The slip was printed and Chris signed it. The clerk asked if he could help with the box. Chris said no, but he could open the door.

The box was awkward to carry. Arriving home he decided that carrying it to the TS building would be difficult. He got the trolley cart, loaded the box on it and wheeled it to the TS building.

He unpacked the model and placed it on his workbench. Sitting at the workbench he began to read the manual. It contained the standard instructions – how to start the model and how to control it with the remote control. One feature he noticed was that there was a separate channel for an additional item he could add to the model. Just what he needed – the switch to control the time travel could be done remotely.

The time dials had to be mounted in the model. The only logical, and large enough space, was the model's roof. An extra 'bonus' was that the roof was held on by snaps. Determining that it would work, he unsnapped it and set it aside. The inside looked large enough for the other parts, but to be sure he measured it - 30 inches long, 10 ½ inches wide and from the inside floor to the roof it was only 5 ½ inches. With the back seat down there was enough space from the front seat to the back door - just enough for a time module, power supply, and barely leaving enough room for the laser and capacitors.

The time modules went in smoothly, and even the capacitors. The lasers, if they were smaller, would solve some of the problems. The biggest problem was the space for the insulator. The only way to make it fit was to install a reduced size one, but it would make the time travel very slow to start as the burst voltage would be a lot less. With no choice, he installed a reduced size insulator. He was working installing the capacitors when Jennifer walked in.

"Is everything going ok?"

"Yes, but I'm having a problem with the lasers and insulator. If I could get some additional space by using fewer lasers, I could fit in a reduced size insulator."

He asked if she had any suggestions. Jennifer kept up with the advancements in the laser area. The article she read the night before was on the advances in laser diodes and there was a new one available, very powerful for its size. The model LAZ-525 had twice the power and was half the size of the LAZ-325 they had used.

"Check with John and see if they're available?"

He picked up the phone and dialed the supplier's phone number. A lady answered, and in a pleasant voice said, "Good afternoon, 'WEST COAST SCIENTIFIC ELECTRONICS SUPPLIES'. How can I direct your call?"

"Is John Blakley there?"

"Yes, one moment please."

A few seconds later the phone rang again. John answered and talked to Chris like they were long lost buddies. They had talked many times before so he was glad to hear from Chris. Chris asked him about the new diodes, LAZ-525 and if they were in stock. John typed the numbers into the computer and after a few seconds said 4 were available from the California warehouse at a price of $971.19 each.

"I'll take all four; can you get them sent by overnight courier?"

John said he could and the total would be $3884.76 plus $12 for shipping. Chris agreed and gave his credit card number. John, being polite and probably a little inquisitive asked how his project was going. Not mentioning actually what he was doing, 'still experimenting on some fuel efficiency ideas' Chris said.

"The authorization is approved; they are on their way, anything else?"

'No, that's all for now, thanks."

"Thank you," John replied and hung up the phone.

He got up and walked over to the bench just as Jennifer was leaving.

The new diodes would get the model functional, but the range would be very limited, probably a few hundred years or so because of the energy it was able to store. He reached for the parts box on a shelf and set it on the table. Scavenging through the box he found the item he needed, date and time indicator just the same as in the TS. The indicator was 7 inches long and ¾ inches wide and would fit inside the moon roof. The moon roof was made of plastic, not very thick. He used a razor knife to mark the area to cutout, drilled holes and cut it with a power hacksaw. The indicator fit snug and he attached it with screws. A ribbon cable 4 feet long coming out of the back of the indicator needed to be attached to the time module. There was plenty of length, enough to take the roof off without having to remove the cable each time. He plugged it into the module.

He installed an 'engage' switch inside the model with a remote receiver so he could operate it from the remote control. He modified the remote control to work the switch and tested it by pressing the switch on the remote - he could see the switch move. It worked fine. Chris continued working on the TS model until there was nothing more he could do. He was missing the diodes and without them he couldn't continue.

It was almost 5:30. If Jennifer hadn't started dinner yet she might want burgers tonight, good time for a barbeque. He left the model where it was and took the keys out of the TS ignition and put them on the workbench. He was content with what he had accomplished today. It's been a lot of work, but soon they're going to be time traveling he thought. Little did he know it would be sooner than he had planned. He went to the door, turned the lights off, locked the door and went to the house.

"Want to barbeque some burgers tonight," Chris said.

"Sure, I haven't started dinner yet, sounds good."

Jennifer brought the plate with the patties and set it on the table beside the barbeque. In the other hand she had a glass of wine.

"The burgers are here on the table – do you want a drink?"

Chris had the barbeque open checking the flame, turned around and said, "Thanks, a beer would be just perfect."

Chris put the burgers on the barbeque sprinkled some seasoning on them and closed the lid.

She went in the house got a beer and brought it to him. He thanked her as he twisted the cap off the bottle and took a drink. She sat down on a chair at the patio table and asked him how the day had gone for him. He explained there were still a few things to do - the new diodes would solve some of the space problems, in a few days it should be done and ready for testing.

The smell of the burgers cooking was hanging in the air. Finally done, he put them on a plate, grabbed his beer and they went into the house.

After eating dinner they talked a little about the time traveling and a vacation at Christmas in California. Not coming to any conclusions by the time they finished dinner they watched some TV and went to bed.

The next morning Chris was up at 7:30, Jennifer stayed in bed a little longer. Just after 9:00 in the morning a delivery truck came up the driveway and a lady carried a package to the front door.

"Parcel for Chris Manlee."

"That's me"

"Sign here and the parcel is yours."

As Chris was signing she commented, "nice place you have here."

"Thanks, we enjoy it."

He handed the pen and pad back and she gave him a copy of what he signed.

"Have a good day." She closed her pad and walked to the truck. The parcel was from the laser diode vendor. Excitedly he shouted to Jennifer that he was going to the TS building - the diodes had just arrived. She responded from the upstairs that if he needed any help to 'just holler'.

"Will do," as he opened the door and walked to the TS building. He unlocked the door, switched on the lights and carried the parcel to the workbench. There were four diodes in the box along with the data sheets that gave the specifications. The power output was twice the capacity and half the size of the ones he had previously installed.

It took him the better part of three days to get the work completed. On the third day in the afternoon it was all completed and ready to set the equipment for a test. The tests lasted a little over an hour and worked perfectly. He was now ready for a REAL time travel test. Jennifer should witness this, he thought. He started to walk to the house to get her not knowing she had just prepared dinner, and was coming to get him. They met at the man door.

"It's ready for testing, do you want to see the time test?"

"Yes," she replied, "but dinner's ready so it'll have to wait."

He was disappointed but said, "ok", and walked back with her to the house. Hastily he ate his dinner. Not much talking was done during dinner except Chris briefly explaining what he wanted to do for the test.

After dinner they left the dishes on the table, and went to the TS building.

Chris explained ......

He'll set the time indicator for August 19, 2004 at 9 pm (2100 hrs), put his wristwatch in it and send it on the time trip. The time on his watch was 8:11 pm, he put it in the model, snapped the roof on. He picked up the remote control, stepped back about five feet to where Jennifer was standing. He was ready for the test. He asked her, "Do you want the honor?"

"No, you go ahead," she said, "It's your design."

He pressed the button on the remote control and initiated the model for the time travel. There was a bright indigo light then the model became transparent and slowly faded until it disappeared.

"Looks like that part worked well," said Jennifer.

"Yes, just have to wait for it to return."

The dishes were still on the table so they went into the house, put them in the dishwasher and cleaned the table. He kept looking at the kitchen clock and at 8:47 pm they went to the TS building and waited patiently for it to materialize. At 9 pm the mini TS started appearing - first transparent, then it materialized. They walked to it. He removed the roof snaps and pulled the wristwatch out, the time was 8:13, two minutes past the time he had put it in the model.

Everything looked ok, except the insulators had some charred marks, like there had been an electrical arc flowing over the insulator.

"Could be a serious problem," Jennifer said as they looked at the insulator.

"Probably not, the insulator I used was smaller than the one in the TS – there wasn't enough room to install the larger one. That's why it took so long to disappear - the burst voltage was reduced."

Jennifer commented that the marks on the insulators looked bad and even had a lot of carbon deposits on them. Chris agreed reluctantly and said he would fix the insulator problem and try again to send the model through time.

CHAPTER 4

Over the years since Chris started on the TS project, the local people became suspicious of what he was experimenting with in his large garage. Due to the suspicious nature of some people, various speculations surfaced from developing alternate forms of energy, building a space ship, harboring space aliens, right up to time travel. The speculations were based on nothing as no one had been inside the building with the exception of Rich and his family.

Two young culprits, probably the most suspicious of all, Mike Donald and Geoff Johnson occasionally parked off the main road, and walked to where they could see some of the inside of the building when the roll up door was open.

Mike worked in a bookstore as a clerk and liked to read science fiction stories. His short brown hair was average length but a little thin. He was in his mid twenties, mild mannered, but did foolish things due to his affiliation with Geoff. Geoff was in his mid twenties and worked in a grocery store as a clerk and shelf stocker. His dark brown hair went half way down his neck. He had a scraggly mustache, receding hairline, was taller than Mike, and in average physical shape from doing physical work in the grocery store.

Mike didn't have a car so Geoff's was used for all the transportation. His car was a small, red four-door hatchback with a low powered engine.

They had been friends since the first grade and were always arguing, mostly about nothing. Mike generally agreed with Geoff, mostly because of Geoff's gruff and unsophisticated nature. Geoff was always looking to make a quick buck and under the impression life owed him something. They got into minor trouble mainly because Geoff was inquisitive as to what other people had and if he could get 'something for nothing'.

Geoff, and Mike to a lesser extent, was especially interested in the Manlee's. Because of the rumors, they imagined all sorts of 'mysterious goings on' in the big garage and drove to the edge of the Manlee's property many times especially at night. Geoff thought about breaking in to see what was there, but not doing so, for one reason or another. They used binoculars to observe the building, the number of doors and the best possible way to get in.

August 25, 2004, that evening, they drove by the Manlee's - the roll up door was open. They parked the car behind a big bush near the main road concealing most of the car from the driveway. Mike grabbed the binoculars as he got out of the car and walked over to a small cluster of trees. Geoff, struggling to get out, followed him.

"Can't see exactly what's in the building but looks like a table with some computers and tools."

"Give me those," Geoff said as he grabbed the binoculars from Mike.

"Owh.......... You didn't have to grab them, my hand was in the strap."

"Looks like computers on a table." He paused and looked a little longer.

Geoff was determined to get into the building to see what the Manlee's had in there. He told Mike that they were going to come back after midnight. Mike was reluctant to come back as he had to work the next day – why not come back on Saturday.

"Big deal, so do I ...... what's so special about Saturday?"

"Don't have to work the next day."

Geoff's idea, as he told Mike, was to use a cutting torch, cut a hole in the door, or if there was a lock, then use the bolt cutters on the lock.

"Cutting a hole isn't a good idea, Geoff."

"How else do we get in ...., the other door faces the house." Geoff continued saying the roll up door was thin metal and it could be cut 'like cheese'.

Mike was still concerned; the Manlee's would know someone had broken in.

They walked back to the car and drove to their favorite burger place.

It was not quite midnight when they went to Geoff's place to get the equipment for the 'visit to the Manlee's garage'. Mike was still a little hesitant, but Geoff in his gruff tone told him they were going to get the cutting torch, the small gas bottles and the bolt cutters.

"Whose cutting set is this?" asked Mike in a soft tone.

"My dad's, he won't miss it .... he's gone for two weeks, welding on a construction site in California."

Geoff grabbed a backpack hanging on the wall. In it was a disposable 35 mm camera, and a flashlight. Grabbing the flashlight, he turned it on, no light. Shaking it, there was a flicker, then a bright light. He turned it off and returned it to the backpack. He reached for the camera; it was dinted, like it had been dropped. He shook it, nothing rattled so he put it back in the backpack.

Mike put the bolt cutters, torch and gas bottles in the bag following Geoff's orders. He struggled to lift the backpack; carried it to the car and set it beside the back fender. He opened the door, got a good grip on the straps, grunted, and lifted it onto the back seat. They got in the car and drove to the Manlee's.

The Manlee's had gone to bed just before 11:00 pm but Chris had trouble getting to sleep. After ten minutes of lying there with his eyes open, he reached for the lamp on the night table beside him and turned it on. Jennifer was facing the opposite way, and didn't stir at all. He took a news magazine off the night table and began reading. Twenty minutes later he was tired enough to sleep so he turned off the light. His mind was still going through the tests done on the TS and how well they went. Eventually he fell into a light sleep, awakening occasionally, but falling back to sleep.

It was just after midnight when Mike and Geoff arrived and parked the car behind a bush.

Mike took the heavy backpack from the backseat and struggling, set it on the ground. The bottles 'clanged'.

"Quiet!"

Mike bent down, then reached around the gas bottles and pulled the flashlight out of the backpack. Geoff took the flashlight and twisted it into his back pocket.

"You comin'?"

Mike stood up and didn't say a word. Grabbing the backpack, struggling he lifted it and swung it around to his back, caught the strap and put it on. There was another 'clang' when the bottles hit together.

Geoff looked at him. "Quiet, what's holding you up? .... Let's get going."

"It's heavy."

"Just get it on and let's go."

They cunningly walked towards the TS building. The night was warm, good moonlight except for the occasional cloud. Mike was walking behind Geoff carrying the heavy backpack. The bottles 'clanged' at nearly every step he took.

"Quiet, you nit. Trying to wake them up?"

Geoff, took his light summer jacket off, opened the backpack and stuffed it between the bottles. Mike continued walking, stumbling a few times, but didn't fall.

They reached the door. Mike was glad to get the backpack off; the shoulder straps were cutting into his shoulders. Geoff tapped the door lightly with his knuckles.

'Knock .... knock' – a light metallic sounded.

"This is going to be a snap to cut through, gimme the bottles and torch." He grinned and reached for the torch and bottles in the backpack.

Mike still didn't like the idea and wanted to look at the other door.

"This is the way were going to get in, stay here," Geoff said grumpily but softly.

"Ok........, Ok ...., let's do it so I can get home."

Mike took the cutting set and goggles out of the backpack and handed them to Geoff. He took the goggles, put them on, but not over his eyes. The hose was attached to the bottles; he turned one of the valves, lit the torch, and then turned the other one on to get a good cutting flame. He slid the glasses over his eyes and started cutting at the bottom near the center of the door. He continued to the top and did the same thing on the other side. He mumbled to Mike, "catch these pieces before they fall", but Mike was looking around the corner towards the house and was too far to hear what Geoff said.

Geoff made the final cut and the pieces fell making a series of clanging sounds when they hit the ground.

"Why didn't you catch them?" There was no response. "Where the hell are you?"

"Over here."

"Why didn't you catch it .... didn't you hear me?"

"No I didn't."

Geoff started to push Mike. He stopped suddenly. "Move this out of the way so we can get in."

They moved the cut out pieces. Mike looked to see if there were lights in the house, but couldn't see anything.

"Look again!"

Mike looked again, no lights. Geoff put his jacket on and went into the building.

"Mike, get in here."

Mike went through the hole in the door. Geoff turned the flashlight on, shining it to find the light switch.

He found the switch, next to the man door and switched the lights on. He put the flashlight on a shelf near the light switch.

Chris, not sleeping soundly, was awakened by the noise. Getting out of bed, he walked to the window. A dim light was coming from the far side of the building. Jennifer, although sleeping rather soundly, stirred a bit but didn't waken. He quietly put on his clothes and went to investigate. There was a light coming from the roll up door but not like the door was open. From the outline it made on the ground, it looked like a large hole. Large pieces of twisted metal lay on the ground. In the building he saw two young men, examining the TS. He went to the man door, got the key out of his pocket and quietly opened it. Inside, he slowly closed the door and hid behind a steel shelf rack and looked for something to use as a weapon. Mike and Geoff didn't see him. On the shelf he found a 2-foot piece of pipe. Chris could see Mike at the back with the door open and Geoff sitting in the driver's seat with the front door open.

Geoff, in the driver's seat, had the ignition switch on and was looking at the indicators and gauges.

"Mike, Look what's here, a new fangled electric vehicle."

Mike closed the back. Walked to where Geoff was looking at the indicators and gauges all lit up.

Chris slipped quietly to the back of the TS, crouched down and looked around the back of the TS to where Mike was standing.

"These dials are strange – they're like a calendar". (He was referring to the time indicators.) "Wonder what they do?"

Mike was a little jumpy, he wasn't sure if the noise woke the Manlee's. "I don't like this, have a feeling somebody is watching us - let's take some pictures and get outta' here."

Geoff said "no"; he wanted to see what the indicators did although he wasn't brave enough to press any buttons, but wanted to see what would happen.

"Don't press anything – We don't want any alarms," said Mike.

Chris, with the pipe in his hand, stepped out from behind the back of the TS. The driver's door was open; Mike could see Chris in the door's mirror.

"Someone's here!" said Mike as he ran for the hole and through it. He grabbed the backpack, with the cutting torch and the bottles and kept on running. The bottles, a little heavy, were dragging on the ground making a scraping noise. Geoff, surprised at seeing Mike run out, didn't know what was happening until he stepped out of the TS and saw Chris coming at him with the pipe in his hand. Geoff lunged at Chris causing the pipe to fly out of his hand and knock over one of the tower computers sitting on the floor. When the computer fell, a cable was strained and some wires broke. Geoff grabbed Chris around the neck and pushed him inside the open door of the TS. Chris fell, hitting his head on the steering wheel. He moved his hand to try and swing at Geoff but hit the 'engage' switch by mistake. The time travel was initiated. Suddenly from the back of the TS there was a bright blue light. Geoff, startled by the light and low-pitched sound, let go of Chris and ran out the hole.

Chris, his head hurting, saw that the TS was initiated for time travel. He had to make a decision – jump out and lose the TS to a different time or stay in it and bring it back. Deciding to go, he closed the door. The indicator was set for August 10, 1971 at 10 am.

This was the time he had previously set to see his parents. Everything started to change around the TS. For brief moments he could see himself and Jennifer moving very fast in the TS building until it was 'un-built'. There was changing of day to night, like turning a light on and off continuously. The orchard trees went through their seasonal changes and the weather changed from rain, sun, occasional snow and hail and back. The changes lasted only seconds.

Geoff caught up to Mike.

"What happened?"

"He attacked me with a piece of pipe. We ended up in the SUV and his hand hit something on the dash - some sort of a switch. The SUV lit up – then a low sound like there was going to be an explosion or something. Why didn't you stay and help me, you nit?"

"I thought you were right behind me, so I took off."

"How could I be behind you when I was still in the SUV?"

"Don't know."

They looked back and could see a blue light fading through the hole in the door, the light disappeared and the normal light shone dimly through. Mike and Geoff were still curious and from this experience were still determined to go back.

"Time to go home," Mike said. Geoff agreed and they put the backpack in the car and drove away.

Chris was in 1971 - the time travel seemed like it had only taken a few minutes.

CHAPTER 5

August 26, 2004. Almost 1:30 in the morning, the clanging bottles eventually woke Jennifer. Suddenly the noise stopped. She squinted at the clock on her night table; it was almost half past one in the morning. She looked at the other side of the bed but Chris wasn't there. Was he still in the TS Building she thought. She got out of bed, looked out the window. There was a faint light on the far side of building. Chris's clothes were gone, is he working on the TS, but why so late? She put on her robe and slippers and walked to the building.

Trying the man door first she found it unlocked and walked in. The lights were on, the TS was gone and a computer was tipped over. She saw the gaping hole in the door. Many thoughts were going through her mind – break in, kidnapping, TS on a time travel, what had happened? What to do - Call the police?

………… Out of the question.

While walking towards the man door, a transparent TS appeared, coming through the wall, turning and settling in its location. The TS started to materialize. Chris was inside it. He opened the door, got out, and walked to her. He had a smile on his face, hugged her and said, "I missed you, dear."

She hugged him, but pulled back slightly; surprised he acted like he hadn't seen her in a long time.

"Where have you been? .... What happened?" she asked in shock.

Chris told her he had been to 1971.

"What happened in here?"

"I heard a noise, like some metal falling to the ground. It woke me up. I came out to check it out. When I looked inside there were two young men. I fought with one of them, my hand hit the 'engage' switch and started the time travel."

"Why didn't you wake me? You could've been hurt."

"Didn't think it would be anything serious."

"It was serious. If both of them had stayed it might have turned out a lot worse."

"Yes, but they didn't," said Chris a little more determined than he should have been.

Chris continued telling her what happened..................

"When I hit the switch, I had to go with the TS or it would have been lost."

She said another could be built. Chris didn't want to as all the work was completed - it would be a setback.

"I've got to put something over the hole in the door, then we'll go inside and I'll explain what happened."

There were some sheets of thin veneer leaning against the wall. He picked one up and carried it to the door, flipped it up against the hole. He asked her if she could hold it while he got the hammer and nails. Jennifer held it in place. He nailed the veneer to the door panels, making a loud noise with each strike. He bent the nails on the other side. It worked, but was a temporary fix.

"I'll get some replacement panels tomorrow and fix it properly. I don't think they'll be back tonight, I told them the police were coming. I don't know if they believed me though."

Chris went to the TS, opened the door, got the keys and pressed 'Lock' on the remote control.

He turned the light off and locked the door as they left.

"Ok, what happened?" she asked, "I'm not going to bed until you've told me everything. I'll make some coffee."

Chris began to explain as they walked to the house ……

He had landed in the same location where he had left from, but in 1971. Some of the area was different. The house was still the same; there was an old garage and one driveway. The orchard had many more trees, almost double what was there now. Luckily, there was no one home. Still slightly dazed, he drove the TS behind the old garage, got out and went into the house - his parents rarely locked the house. He looked at the fireplace mantel and it had numerous pictures. Several memories - one especially was a picture of him and his father on a fishing trip, where they had caught so many fish it seemed like the fish were 'jumping in the boat'.

A car pulled up to the front of the house. Peeking out of the window, it was his parent's 1969 station wagon. He hurriedly went out the back door and stood at the back corner of the house. How does he approach his parents – what does he say? His father got out of the driver's side. His mother got out, opened the back door and helped his brother out of a baby chair. Chris, as a young boy, wasn't there because he spent most of August at a summer camp. A strange feeling came over him - his parents were younger than he was.

How to approach the situation - say he's their son from the future or he had a problem with his truck and was looking for a phone to call a garage. He weighed his options - a problem with his truck would probably be best for now.

Walking from the back of the house, he said "hello."

"Hello, are you looking for someone," his mother said.

Chris told her he had a problem with his truck and needed to phone a garage.

His mother looked at him, feeling she knew him or at least felt she had seen him somewhere before. Was he staying at neighbors she asked? Chris replied kindly, "just passing through."

"The phone is in the house, in the kitchen," his father said.

"Thanks," he replied and walked with them into the house and directly to the phone in the kitchen. His parents were surprised – it was as if he knew its location. Chris dialed in six random numbers, but didn't dial a seventh number. He paused for ten seconds, said hello, and talked into the phone explaining he had a problem with his truck, where it was located and if someone could come out and look at it. After about thirty seconds, the phone rang three times, three high pitched tones, each higher than the previous and a recording came on – 'were sorry your call did not go through, will you please try your call again'. He hesitated a few seconds than said, "thanks, I'll wait for your call."

He hung up the phone and walked into the living room.

"A nice place you have here. Been here long?"

"Yes, we've been here for almost five years .... is someone coming to fix your truck?" his father questioned.

Chris told him the service station would have a truck available in a few hours and would phone before they came. He changed the subject and asked his mother their son's name, knowing what it was. She replied 'Rich' and he has an older brother away at summer camp.

It was noon, his mother asked him if he'd like some lunch. Chris said 'yes' and thanked them for their hospitality. His mother returned fifteen minutes later with some sandwiches. She fed Rich as well and when he finished eating she picked him up. "I'm going to the orchard to pick some fruit."

"Need any help?" his father asked.

"No, I'll be fine. I want to check the garden also."

After they finished eating, Chris got up, walked over to the mantel and pointed to one of the pictures.

"Is this your son? Looks like a fine boy."

The picture was the one of him and his father on a fishing trip. His father replied yes and explained about the summer camp.

"What do they do there?"

"Swimming, hiking, nature and science field trips. What he likes the most is experimenting with electronics and would probably be a scientist or engineer some day."

Chris thought, he's sure right – 'hit the nail on the head'.

They spent the afternoon talking about the weather, current events, camping and fishing. At 5:10 his mother came back into the house and asked Chris if he would like to stay for dinner. Didn't look like the service station was going to get there to fix his truck, maybe he should phone again.

"I can set another plate, if you like."

Chris said 'yes' to the dinner, but was slow getting up, hoping another conversation would start with his father so he wouldn't have to phone again. It was 6 pm, Chris said he would phone tomorrow, and look for a place to stay tonight.

The smell of the cooking food gradually drifted into the living room where Chris and his father were sitting. Soon his mother called them to 'come and eat'. Chris sat at one end and his father at the other with his mother to the side closest to the stove. Chris had a strange characteristic when he ate. He would cut his steak with a fork in his right hand then switch the fork to his left hand to eat.

His mother noticed and commented that their son ate the same way.

"Just a habit, I guess." Chris said.

"What did you say your name was?"

"Chris."

She said their son's name was Christopher, but they called him Chris.

It started again - going through his mind – should he tell his parents he's their son from the future? With little hesitation - yes, might as well get it over with because this was the purpose of his trip.

"I should have told you before but didn't know if you'd believe me".

Chris explained he was their son from the future and he had built a time traveling machine.

Looking at his father, "it's probably similar to yours, mine is built into a small truck."

"I'm from 2004," he said, "and the technology to build a time traveling machine was now available. He said eagerly his wife's name is Jennifer and Rich and his wife Donna have a son named John.

"I still live in this house, but Rich and his family live in California. .... Jennifer and I don't have any children, been too busy with our careers and the time traveling machine."

Should he tell his parents they weren't living and what will happen to them?

His father, still skeptical, questioned further.

"How do we really know your Chris from the future – from what year .... 2004?" his father asked.

Chris responded yes, telling him he remembered, as a young boy, his father's experimenting with a small time travel machine.

"I don't have a working model, some of the components are difficult to get."

"I'd like to see your design." His father leaned slightly forward and asked where his machine was.

"Behind the garage."

Chris said he was interested in the design because it was a lot smaller.

Still skeptical, his father did not volunteer his design ideas. Deciding to test him on how well he remembered a camping incident, he said .... "In June of 1970 we went on a camping trip to the mountains."

"We were supposed to go on a short hike."

"What else happened?"

Chris replied, "We were lost for three days, fortunately we had warm jackets, the water canteen and some candy bars."

Chris told him they got cold and had to huddle together to keep warm. They didn't have any matches and couldn't make a fire.

"We used some branches to keep warm but that didn't work very well."

His father asked how they were found and his mother started to explain. After two days she got worried, called the park rangers, because every evening they would go to the lodge and phone. She was concerned something had happened when the rangers found the sleeping bags unused the next day.

"They're still down in the basement, haven't used them and it's been over a year," his father said.

Getting some confidence, he said they could look at his notes after dinner but there were still many items to solve. During dinner they talked about Chris, what he did when growing up to 1971. Chris didn't say much about the time after 1972 because of the fatal accident.

His mother asked if he went to college and what he studied.

"Yes, studied electrical engineering, more of the electronics."

"What type of work do you do," asked his father.

Chris explained nearly all his time is spent working on the time traveling machine but before that he had designed computer chips, or as they called them in 1971 'integrated circuits'.

"Integrated circuits have been under development since 1958. Just last year they started to sell dynamic RAM memory," his father said.

"There's going to be a microprocessor chip released in November," said Chris, "it could help in your design if you need a small computer," said Chris.

"It's a four bit unit. You know, it was .... is going to be used by NASA."

His father said the transistor and integrated circuits were great developments and electronics has progressed significantly since Schockley and his group developed the transistor in the late forties. He asked Chris why he became interested in time travel.

"My interest was because of your experimenting."

Chris said he remembered as a boy, being told by him of all the interesting possibilities of time travel.

"It was only on a theoretical basis, no one has developed one, except for you as far as I know. The equipment and energy required are not available so I compromised on some of it," his father explained.

He had trouble finding a computer device and a reliable energy source such as nuclear. There was some at the university, but very difficult to get because it was kept locked up - in the wrong hands it could be dangerous.

"I use laser capacitors to create the energy for mine," responded Chris.

"Lasers are being used for many applications since Theodore Maimam developed the first one in his lab in the 1960s." replied his father. "Did you know Einstein proposed the theory on them in 1917?"

"Yes, he was probably the smartest scientist we have known for his workable theories."

His father commented he was not aware of lasers being used to create energy sources, they used a lot of energy. Chris said the lasers of the future are small, some even operate from flashlight batteries, but those don't have much power.

"I can understand, the technology since the 1960s has already changed dramatically," replied his father.

After dinner Chris and his father went into the basement. The sketches and notes were on a large table along with a slide rule and a small electronic calculator.

He picked up the slide rule and told Chris most of his calculations were done on it, had an electronic calculator but all it did was the four basic functions of add, subtract, multiply and divide. Chris said he had heard of a slide rule, but never used one.

"They're good for doing calculations, but not as accurate as a calculator."

Chris said he had one that was like a small computer.

"Could use something like that," his father said.

"I have access to a mainframe computer at the University, when it's not being used I do some of my calculations on it."

His father was a Physics Professor at the local state university and did some programming on the main frame mostly for solving physics problems, of which calculations for the time travel machine were 'snuck in' occasionally. He needed a computer to control the energy flow, and had thought of abandoning the portable time traveling machine because a small computer was not available.

"I'll show you the sketches but there still are many things to solve."

His father got the sketches. Some missing items were still needed but a description of the parts and they're function was described by each item. Chris commented the unit was very similar to the one he developed, except for the energy supply being controlled differently. His father's unit didn't use an energy boost, so the travel would start slow, and would take longer to reach the destination.

Chris was still wondering how to tell his parents about the fatal auto accident. He asked his father to leave the notes and sketches behind some loose wall boards by the stairs – it was into a 'crawl space' not exposed to the outside.

"Yes, but the design is not practical, never considered hiding it," his father said.

Chris explained if anything should happen the notes and sketches could be thrown out.

"Can you explain that?" asked his father.

"Who knows where your drawings and prototypes will end up if anything happens."

His father agreed, puzzled a bit, not knowing why. After spending hours in the basement, they went upstairs.

Chris, still wanting to warn his parents of the impending danger, "Be careful in the near future on ---." He stopped, but would try and bring it up later.

His mother interrupted - what happens in the future is destiny and shouldn't be changed. Chris explained he could save their lives. His father interrupted - the past should not be changed or altered regardless of the reason.

"Ok, I won't mention it any more," but he was still determined to tell at a more appropriate time later - he hoped.

In the evening his mother said he could sleep in 'his' bedroom. She was still overwhelmed by him being her son.

"Still hard to believe it's you .... you know what I mean."

Chris and his father went outside to the TS. He drove the TS around to the front of the garage. It's a nice looking truck, "looks like a Suburban," his father commented.

Chris said in 2004 they're called an 'SUV', or a sports utility vehicle.

"I call this one The Time Surveyor or TS, because it's a special one," replied Chris.

"The time travel equipment is mainly in the back," as he opened the back of the SUV.

When the back was open he could see the insulator was charred with electrical arc tracking.

Chris explained he built a time traveling machine in a model and it had the same problem. The probable cause, he continued, is the high burst voltage to accelerate the TS into the time travel mode.

"After the initial burst, it goes down to a lower voltage so there isn't a problem. It's like getting a boost, then sort of coasting."

"Maybe you can use some of my design, it doesn't use a burst voltage," his father said.

Chris showed him the controls on the front dash and explained the three sets of indicators, the gauges and the switch to initiate time travel. The surrounding changes, when time traveling, were incredible he told his father.

"You can see buildings being 'un-built', the seasonal changes - rain, hail, sunny, even snow, trees growing, bearing fruit, then bare, night and day changing very rapidly – like turning a flashlight on and off."

It was getting late and dark so they decided to go into the house.

CHAPTER 6

August 11, 1971. It was after 7:30 in the morning, Chris awoke and lingered for a while, looking at the posters and toys. It brought back memories, he felt comfortable sleeping in 'his' bed. At 8:00 am his mother called him. Breakfast would be ready in twenty minutes. Chris got up, did his things in the bathroom and came out. She was just putting breakfast on the table – scrambled eggs, potatoes and bacon. They all sat down and talked about current (1971) news and a little of what was news in the future. After they had eaten, Chris asked them if they would like to see some more of his time traveling machine. His father said yes, but his mother had other things to do.

"I have to give Rich a bath and do the dishes - you two go and I'll come out later."

Chris and his father walked to the TS.

"I'd like to design an abort control, but it could take some time to design. When the unit starts, the cycle has to complete, if it doesn't, I don't know what time period I would end up in." His father wasn't sure either, as he hadn't gotten to that part on his design yet.

"What's this?" his father asked, pointing to the GPS system.

"It's called a Global Positioning System," Chris said, "in the future there would be satellites launched having a band for civilian use, the GPS would display the coordinates if the satellites were in orbit."

"I remember, the Navy tested a positioning system in the early '60s. It was called something like 'TRANSIT' and later in '67 they launched a 'TIMATION' series."

His father continued, "it was used only for the navigation of Navy ships and subs."

"Those systems were the forerunners of the system used in 2004," Chris said. "The government finally allowed a system with higher accuracy to be available to the public, in fact you can buy very accurate hand held device. It would have been good having a system like that when we got lost."

"Yes, it would have been nice to have one of those if they had the satellites up," said his father.

"I'd like to build it into the TS time system so I could dial in coordinates and travel to that position. The problem is it won't work very far in the past and I don't know how far in the future it'll work." Looking at the indicators, his father asked him how he sets the return coordinates. He explained the return is manually set. The return was set after the time he left, showing his father how he set it by the thumbwheels to August 26, 2004 at 1:45 am.

"Drive your TS into the garage incase someone comes along. – It would be difficult explaining what this is."

The garage wasn't on the Manlee's property in the future. It was in need of a lot of repair so his aunt and uncle had it torn down after his parents died in 1972.

Chris got into the TS and drove it into the garage, just as his mother came out. Chris showed her the TS and explained some of the items on it.

"Very nice, she commented. "It's looks as practical as the station wagon we have, except more trunk space." As she was looking in the back she asked what the big equipment was.

"That's the main time travel unit, it has the power unit and the control modules."

Chris went on to explain its functions. It was the same as his father's, except the power unit was different. After he finished giving his mother the 'tour', he asked his father if he knew where he could get an insulator to fit the TS.

"Insulators like the one you need are probably in the maintenance shacks along the high voltage transmission lines. You know the lines about five miles from here. You can also try the local electrical supply store but I don't think they'd have them in stock, they can probably be ordered though."

It was late in the afternoon, so Chris said he would check it out tomorrow. Actually he wanted to delay it so he could spend more time with his parents. In the evening his father talked about some recent and future events.

"Do you remember Apollo 11 in 1969 when they landed on the moon?"

"I do vaguely, was it on TV?" asked Chris.

"Yes, and Apollo 13 .... those astronauts sure came through .... they must train them for those situations. How far did they extend the space travel, did they go to any other place, such as Mars?"

Chris told him the space flights lasted to Apollo 17 in 1972 and no more manned flight were made to the moon or anywhere after that.

"Although, they do build an international space station later this century and into the next. NASA did send some unmanned missions to Mars, some were lost but some made it and transmitted pictures back to earth."

The pictures sent back from Mars were incredible he said and added, showing a lot of detail. Chris further explained that there are manned flights planned, but way after 2004.

"We got involved in the Vietnam War in the mid sixties and they started peace accords in 1969," said his father, "is there still a war going on?"

"No, a peace accord was signed in '73, but the war continued a few years after that. The North took over the South and they continued invading some of the surrounding countries."

"Where there any other major conflicts?"

"There were other conflicts, but probably the most prevalent one was with Iraq in the early 1990s and 2003. There were some serious ignominious terrorist attacks also – the worst being the total devastation of the world trade center in New York on September 11, 2001."

"It's getting late," his father said. "You'll have to tell me more about these future events tomorrow."

Chris said he would be happy to.

The next morning he would have to find and install a new insulator, or chance a return trip with the possibility

of the insulator failing. His preference was to find one, either at the electrical supply store or 'borrow' one from the utility.

CHAPTER 7

August 12, 1971. Chris woke up at 8:00 am, but laid in bed for a while. He again looked around the room at the toys and posters on the wall.

His thoughts were that he should bring Jennifer and Rich and his family here. A few minutes later he got up, did his morning requirements and went to the kitchen. The breakfast his mother made was excellent as usual. Chris was just finishing his second cup of coffee when his father entered the kitchen.

"We can leave whenever you want for the electrical store." His father said.

Chris took one last sip and was ready to go. They took his dad's car.

The countryside hadn't change much in thirty years. There were a few less homes than in 2004.

After driving for a while, his father asked him about his comment yesterday that the manned flight stopped at Apollo 17 – For what reason?

"They developed a new type of rocket to do more unmanned flights, probably exploration flights - the costs of the manned flights were very expensive."

Chris hesitated a moment and mentioned about the microprocessor he told his father about yesterday.

"Yes, the four bit one?"

"It was used by NASA in a series of rockets called the Pioneer ......it'll be the first spacecraft to pass through the asteroid belt."

"When was it launched?"

"In seventy two"

They arrived at the electrical store, drove into a parking spot and got out of the car.

"There's been a lot of progress since Sputnik went up in '57," his father said as they walked to the store. "The advancements in twenty years of landing a man on the moon were enormous - what you said about them not pursuing it further for other moon trips is disappointing."

"After they went to the moon, the technology to travel the other distances, such as, Mars just wasn't there."

They reached the door, went up to the counter and Chris noticed the nametag on the clerk. The clerk's name was Jim and he asked him if he had any high voltage insulators, similar to the type the electrical utility uses.

"What voltage are you looking at?"

"What is the highest you have available?"

There were three big binders lying just behind the counter.

Jim opened the third one thumbed through the index to the listing of insulators. He found them on page 227. He took the catalog out of the rack and showed Chris what was available.

"These go to 25 KV .... here's one to 50KV."

"Looks like these are the highest rating; there isn't much call as they're usually used only by the electrical utility."

"They buy direct from the manufacturer."

"How many do you want?" asked Jim.

"Just inquiring, but thanks for your help," replied Chris.

"Ok, let me know if we can help you with anything else."

As they walked out, his father said, "The only place you can get one would be at the maintenance shack along the electrical lines."

"Yes, but I'd have to 'borrow' one."

Chris could take a chance with the old insulator and replace it when he got home but if it failed, he could end up in some unknown time period, after 1971, stranded with a TS that didn't work. His father agreed that it would be better to have a new insulator that was sure to get him home.

"When we get back, I'll drop you off, take the TS and go along the transmission line - hopefully there'll be one I can use in one of the shacks."

"That's your decision, but at least a new one will get you back to your time," his father said.

Chris got out of the car and into the TS. His mother was outside with Rich. His father walked next to them. Chris thought that getting the insulator shouldn't be a problem and he'd be back in a short time. What could happen, but if something did he would see them again, maybe with Jennifer, Rich and his family.

"Be careful. Do you want me to come with you?" his father asked. Chris replied no and that he shouldn't be to long.

They waved as Chris drove off, not knowing if this would be the last time they would see him on this trip or ever. Chris gave a couple of quick 'beeps' on the horn and waved. He went down the main road until arriving at the turn to the transmission line service road. He drove for five miles, the road was bumpy and dusty with ruts so deep he didn't have to drive, just let the ruts direct the TS. After a few miles he came to a small building - it looked like a maintenance shack. The door was open, and a crew was working in the area. A utility truck was parked a hundred yards from the shack with the driver's door open, no one was in or near it, as far as he could tell. He parked the TS about twenty feet from the shack and cautiously went inside – no one was there. He went to the stock shelves to search for an insulator. There were two types on the shelves. He grabbed the one with the highest rating, took it to the TS. Should he see if it will fit – yes, there's no one around so he should be able to. He opened the back, got some tools from a metal box in the back, took the cover off the power unit and removed the old insulator. Both the old and the new one were the same size, what luck, so he installed it and replaced the cover. Since it was a perfect fit, it only took about ten minutes. This one should last the trip back he thought. He put the tools away and grabbed the old insulator, closed the door and threw the insulator next to the shack. As he was about to get in the TS a worker walked around the corner of the shack.

"What are you doing here ......are you looking for someone?"

Chris, surprised, said. "I'm trying out my new SUV on these roads."

"What's a SUV?" said the worker.

"It's a four wheel drive."

He saw the old insulator lying on the ground and asked if Chris was in the shack.

"Uh .... no .... yes," said Chris.

He pointed to the old insulator. "Where'd that come from?"

Chris thought he'd 'better get out'a there'. He jumped into the TS, turned the ignition key 'ON' and moved the switch handle to return to 2004.

The maintenance worker, stood there for a few seconds then walked towards the TS. A blue light came from the TS, he stopped about ten feet away, saw it fade, and then it was gone.

He looked around and couldn't believe what had just happened.

Better not tell anyone was his first reaction - probably wouldn't believe me anyway he thought.

Traveling back Chris could hear arcing from the insulator.

"Dam! Hope it lasts for the burst. Can't go on another trip with this problem."

As the TS settled out of burst mode the arcing stopped, but there was a slight odor that smelt like burnt wiring. He was concerned but what could he do – just ride the time travel out.

Approaching 2004, the TS started to coast, almost like it was floating. As it drifted it was transparent, almost like a ghost and was moving to the TS building floating over the land. It was early in the morning. A car with two young men was traveling along the main road just past the Manlee home. The driver saw a dim, glowing object floating along the landscape and moving towards them. The transparent, ghostly TS continued floating at a fast pace and passed in front of the car. The driver, not knowing what it was, swerved into a shallow ditch.

"Did you see that," the driver said.

"What was it?"

"Don't know, could have been a UFO or something."

"Did we imagine it - was it real?"

"Don't know."

Chris saw what had happened and was concerned they might say something. Would anyone believe them anyway?

The TS continued floating through the building wall turned and settled in the landing spot inside the building.

And Chris continued telling Jennifer ....

"When the TS started to materialize, I saw you."

"I was sure happy to be back."

CHAPTER 8

August 26, 2004. They were both exhausted after Chris finished telling her all that had happened – it was after 4 in the morning. He had wanted to say 'good bye' to his parents and wasn't happy not telling them about the car accident.

"You're lucky to make it back with the problem you had."

Chris hadn't thought much more about it – the insulator problem, but a slight sweat came upon him as he didn't know what would have happened if it had failed. He'd have to recheck the insulator. Something else he had to do was check behind the stairs for some sketches and notes his father left there – he hoped.

"I'll go with you." Jennifer said, somewhat excited.

In the basement Chris removed the loose boards and found two large boxes covered in dust.

He carried the boxes to a table and set them down.

The first box he opened had sketches and notes. He opened the other box. Inside it was a prototype of his father's time traveling device – "wait, there's two," Chris said.

He took a time traveling device out of the box and examined it to some extent. It was small, like a backpack, about 8 inches high, 5 inches wide and 4 inches deep. It was designed to wear on the front, with adjustable straps going around the shoulders, crossed at the back and returned to the front where they were clipped together at the waist. On the top section there were two indicators and a push button to the right side of each. A protective collar encased the sides of the push buttons and extended a half-inch above them. This was to protect them from being pressed accidentally. The indicators were smaller than in the TS. There were small rotary knobs below each indicator, but the year could only be set to four digits, not the same as the TS with its six-digit setting. He had labeled each button. The top indicators were labeled 'Start T Trip' and the one beside the bottom labeled 'Return T Trip'. There was an 'ON - OFF' switch in the bottom left corner. He turned the switch 'ON' and the time indicators lit up.

"It still works after all this time." Turning it 'OFF', he placed it back in the box.

In the other box, there was an envelope inside, "it's addressed to you and me and it's from dad."

"What does he write?" asked Jennifer.

Chris began to read the letter ....

August 20, 1971

Dear Chris and Jennifer,

It was very nice to see you Chris. We didn't know where you went, so we assumed you had gone back to 2004. We don't know what the danger was you spoke of, but prefer not to know. I will keep putting my work on the time device in this spot so you can get it in the future should anything happen to me. From our conversation Jennifer seems to be a fine woman. Tell Rich when you see him that mom and I enjoyed your telling us how well he was doing and about his family.

Love to you all,

Dad

He added another sheet to the letter,

March 19, 1972

I have been working on the time Traveling device and will continue to put the progress here. Your ideas have helped me get this far, especially letting me know the microprocessor was being available last November. I used three, the ram memory was what I needed. It is close to being completed, except for the computer.

Love to you all,

Dad

And a final one

MAY 19, 1972

I have all the programming done. My time indicator is only four digits and not six like your time traveling machine. I've calculated that it can go about 8000 years either in the future or past. I based this on the fact that the circuits got too hot and could fail unless they could be cooled down. Short trips of a few thousand years should work quite well. I will be testing it in a few days. If all works well, we will see you in the future. I built a second one as a backup, or for mom to use. It is not totally finished, just need to install some additional parts. Mom hasn't expressed a desire to time travel, but is interested in coming to see you, Jennifer and Rich and his family.

Love to you all,

Dad

Jennifer got a little emotional after hearing the letters. "I would have liked to meet them," she replied.

Chris, emotionally also, said his father was a good man and his mother was good in that she supported him in all things.

"They got along tremendously."

Strangely, the day after the last note they died in a car accident and he never got a chance to test his invention Chris expressed, and not too strongly - that maybe they could go back in time to see them. It was strange although that his parents were younger than he was. She didn't think traveling back would be a good idea, but was open to discussing it later.

"I'm sure tired," she said, "we should get some sleep and look at these later in the morning."

They got up just before noon, had some breakfast and went to the basement. Chris looked in the box at the prototypes again. They appeared to be in good condition even after all the years being in the basement - a little dusty though. He put the box with the prototypes back under the step and replaced the boards.

He took the box of sketches to the TS building. Jennifer opened the man door. Pulling up some chairs they sat at the table where Chris took the papers out of the box, shook them to get the dust off and placed them on the table. There were thirty to forty folded sheets lying on top of some large notebooks. He removed the sheets and saw three notebooks labeled 1, 2, and 3 with dates on them. Unfolding each sketch, he placed them on top of each other. The only items questionable were the computer chip and the memory for the program. It appeared his father had solved the problems, but with RAM memory, if power was lost, it would be erased. The sketches showed the power supply was nuclear, and should be functional for a long time. The computer chips were old, the first type made.

"Wonder where he got the nuclear material - that would have been very difficult to get back then, probably even now."

Chris looked at the design; he could improve it by using a more powerful computer chip and flash memory. He didn't have to do that now though because they would be functional the way they are. He had to divert his priority to getting a new insulator installed. Later he could analyze the notes and drawings to see if he could improve the design with newer components.

Chris kept up to date with advances in the electrical and electronics field by reading the journals - occasionally. He didn't pay particular attention to many new products but had a good memory on what was in the journals. In one of them just recently, he had read about a new insulator made out of a porcelain material with a high rating for its size. At the file cabinet he removed the three most recent issues and looked until he found the article on the insulators. At the end of the article there was an address and phone number. He phoned the company and was able to place an order and asked for it to be couriered overnight.

The next morning he received the package and took it to the TS building. Opening the back of the TS he looked at the position of the existing one. The new insulator was shorter, but wider than the one now installed.

Removing the clear shields from around the power unit, he began to modify the position. After a few hours he had the new one in place and installed the shield around it. He was also concerned that bumping the time travel switch had caused the TS to initiate. To prevent this from happening again he added a push button that would have to be pressed before the switch would work.

After he finished it was time to test the power supply.

He placed the keys in the ignition, turned it 'ON' but didn't start the engine. The control modules and dash instruments lit up. He tested the power supply and it worked well – would this solve the arcing problem? He was confident it would.

It was getting late but Chris still wanted to look at his father's notes.

Mike and Geoff hadn't given up on their curiosity of what the SUV (TS) could do. The blue light, which came from it, must have been for something. Their curiosity was heightened, especially Geoff's. What if it was a time traveling machine? If so they could use it to go to the future and get some ideas on how to make some money – possibly on the stock market, sports betting, lotteries or whatever - that was Mike's idea. They needed another look at the SUV (TS) and if it was a time traveling machine- take it to the future.

"There weren't any police that I could see - he didn't call them," Geoff said. "We're going there TONIGHT – after dark! .... We'll see what's so special about that SUV."

"Ya, let's do it," replied Mike.

CHAPTER 9

August 27, 2004. It was evening and Mike and Geoff drove to the Manlee's, parked the car in the same place, behind the bushes. Geoff opened the glove box, took out a pair of pliers and a blade screwdriver. That's all they were taking Geoff said. They got out of the car; Geoff locked it (one of the few times he did), walked to a better viewing area and could see hints of light coming through the hole. The veneer didn't cover it totally.

"Come on, let's go," said Geoff as he grabbed Mike.

Noiselessly they walked towards the TS building. Without incidence they got there and peeked in through an uncovered piece of the hole. They could see Chris looking at something on the table. They moved to the man door, it was unlocked so they quietly opened it, went in and hid behind some shelves. The door made a 'click' when it closed; Chris turned around and called, "is that you Jennifer?"

No answer.

"Anybody there?" he asked. No answer. Must be the wind or my imagination he concluded.

He turned around, continuing to look at the sketches.

Geoff and Mike spoke softly ....

"We'd better go, come back when he's not here," said Mike.

"We're going to grab him and tie him up," said Geoff.

They had to look for something to tie him up with – rope, but where would they find some. They scanned the shelf to see what was on it and saw some duct tape.

"This'll work."

"We can get into bad trouble doing this," said Mike.

"Don't think they'd report it. Probably doing something illegal if they didn't call the police before."

"Don't know - let's come back some other time."

"No! We're here, we're doing it."

"Ok", Mike said reluctantly.

Geoff walked towards Chris, almost tip toeing, with Mike hesitantly following him. As they approached Chris, Geoff stepped on a piece of wood or something similar lying on the floor, just a few feet from Chris.

'Cr .... ack'

Chris heard the noise and turned around.

Geoff lunged at Chris. As they fell, Chris hit his head on the table as he slid to the floor. Geoff got up and could see Chris wasn't moving.

"Is he dead?" questioned Mike.

Geoff put his head to Chris's chest and listened.

"He's still breathing, he'll be ok."

"He got cut on the head. Not much blood. He'll be ok."

"Do ya think we should leave him like this, what if he dies?"

Geoff told him to go over to the rack and see if he could find some rags or paper towels. Mike went over and looked on the rack. He grabbed a couple of clean rags and brought them to Geoff.

He lifted Chris's head up; Mike folded two up and put them under the cut.

"Go get another so I can wipe my hands."

Mike walked over, picked up a clean rag and gave it to Geoff. He wiped his hands and threw the rag down beside Chris.

"There, - satisfied, he'll be ok."

"Ya, he's going to have a bad headache when he wakes up," replied Mike.

They turned their attention to the TS. Geoff opened the door on the driver's side and got in while Mike climbed in on the passenger side. Geoff turned the ignition key on and the gauges and indicators lit up. They turned around, looked at the power module, or what they could see of it in the back and questioned what it was. After spending a few minutes looking and discussing it, they turned to the front. The indicators were lit up. Geoff was tempted to play with the thumbwheels, but didn't.

"Those sure look like some kind of calendar," said Mike. "This one", as he touched the upper one, "got some dial setters on it," as he started to move the thumbwheels.

The 2004 was changed to a 2104. He left the month as '08'. Moving the day thumbwheels, he ended up with a '05' and finally adjusted the time to 10 am. The date to travel was set at August 5, 2104 at 10 am - for no particular reason.

Geoff recalled that Chris hit the switch with his arm and everything happened – the whine and the bright blue light coming from the back of the TS. He pushed the switch handle up and nothing happened.

"Maybe we're supposed to press this button," as he pushed the 'engage' button - nothing happened.

Chris started to regain consciousness, with the TS door still open he could see two people.

"It was simple last time, the switch was pushed up like this," and as he did the time traveling machine started.

The blue light came from the back and a hum started.

"What's happening," said Mike.

"It looks like we just started a time travel or something."

"Let's get out of here."

"No, close the doors and lets see what happens," and he grabbed Mike who was trying to get out the door. Mike just sat there – he was frightened, probably more petrified at what was happening.

Geoff once again, this time demanding, told him to close the door. Mike closed the door like a frightened child. Actually they both were frightened - Geoff didn't show it as much as Mike, but they continued to sit in the TS. The TS then started fading for its destination. Lying on his back Chris tried to sit up but as he did there was a pain at the back of his head. He moved to his left and slowly used his arms to lift himself up. After sitting up he moved his head from side to side then placed his left hand at the back of his head where he felt some swelling. It felt wet. He pulled his hand back and there was a small amount of blood on it. Struggling to stand he saw the rags on the floor – the ones from under his head. At least they didn't let me bleed to death Chris thought.

Still a little shaky he went over to the computer and checked to see the date set in the TS.

August 5, 2104 but the arrival time was blank.

Wonder why they picked that date - no time display, should have fixed that darn cable he thought. How was he going to get the TS back? He could get his father's time travel devices tested and working, to go to the future and bring it back. How was he going to deal with Geoff and Mike knowing about the TS when and if he brought them back? There was another problem – the changing weather when time traveling. He would have to get some sort of a protective suit.

One good thing was with the TS tracker was activated and he would be able to locate it in the future. The top priority now is to get his father's time traveling devices tested and ready for a trip to the future.

CHAPTER 10

August 27, 2004. It was very late in the evening when Mike and Geoff entered into the time travel. They briefly saw Chris and Jennifer walking in and out of the building at a very fast pace, almost like the fast forward on a VCR, the lights going on and off as they entered and left. A few seconds later Chris and Jennifer put on some full coverage suits, and disappeared. They didn't think much of it and started experiencing the same visual sensations of the surrounding changes as Chris did.

There was some arcing noise, not as severe as when Chris traveled, they didn't pay attention to it – assuming it was normal. After a short while the arcing stopped, the building continued to deteriorate; only parts of the walls were standing. Night, day and weather changes passed at a rapid rate. A period occurred where the area seemed dry for a long time. As the target date approached, the TS slowed down and came to a complete stop – it had materialized in the future.

The time indicator displayed the destination date – August 5, 2104. It was a warm day and sunny at 10:00 in the morning.

"What happened?" asked Geoff. He looked around and saw only the remains of the TS building. Parts of the walls were standing, the roof was gone and only some support trusses remained. Both doors were lying on the ground.

"Don't know, but if the date is correct on this indicator, we're in 2104."

They looked around at the TS building. It was almost totally deteriorated, a few walls partially standing and the doors lying on the ground.

"You're right," said Geoff. One of the few times he acknowledged Mike was right.

Mike wanted to see what their homes look like now and who's living in them. Geoff wasn't interested as he said that that was a hundred years ago.

"You wouldn't know them from a hole in the ground," said Geoff.

"Uh...... h, would be interesting to see our future families."

"Ok, fifteen minutes is all you have."

Geoff started the engine, drove over what was left of the roll up door and down the driveway. It was cracked in many places and the ride was bumpy. Geoff turned onto the main road and drove to where Mike had lived a hundred years before. The streets had changed, some looked like the old neighborhood with many houses having paint peeling and fences broken.

Mike's house looked almost the same, except it was painted a different color. It had a large yard and a white fence three feet high that needed painting. It surrounded only the front of the yard. They got out of the TS, opened the gate and walked into the yard. Geoff kept reminding Mike that he had 15 minutes and that they were going to be out of there.

"Ok, ok, just want to see who lives here."

Two children were in the yard. One was in the corner playing in a sand box. The other, a girl about 5 years old, had just come out the front door and walked up to them. She asked them their names as she cuddled a doll that looked almost alive by its facial movements.

"I used to live here - and what's your name," Mike said.

"Cathy, where do you live?"

"I live far away from here." Mike was intrigued with the doll she was holding and asked her what it was.

"It's a pal doll, got it for my birthday yesterday."

Mike touched the doll. "It feels like real skin," he said as he looked at Geoff.

"Ya", replied Geoff, "your time's a tickin', let's get going."

Mike looked back at the girl. "Is your mom home?"

"She's in the house."

She stood the doll on the ground and said. "Walk with me."

The doll responded with a girlish mechanical voice. "YES CATHY, WE CAN GO FOR A WALK." It started to move, not totally mechanical, but walked almost like the girl towards the sand box.

Mike, amazed at what the doll did, commented he should get one for his little sister. Geoff in his gruffy manner asked how he was going to pay for it.

"Don't know, maybe we can change our money into what they have now."

"Better get going to a bank," Geoff said, but Mike still wanted to see who was living there. At the door, Mike rang the doorbell.

A lady in her early thirties opened the door. "What can I do for you?"

Mike explained - looking for the Donald family. She hadn't heard of anyone living there before by that name, 'been here for almost 30 years'. Her parents owned the house before that. Mike asked if he could talk to her them. She told him they lived in a condo on the other side of the city.

"Nobody lived here before that .... probably at least 10 years .... people abandoned the homes during the drought and the recession in the early forties."

His family, a hundred years ago, used to live here – did she know of any way to find out where they went. She questioned why he was interested in his family a hundred years ago. Lost for an explanation, Mike paused a few seconds and said 'genealogy'. Her only suggestion was that he could go to city hall and search the records.

A man drove up and parked behind the TS. Waving at the children he walked to Geoff, "nice antique vehicle you have there - is it gas run - not many places sell gasoline any more."

"Ya, its gas run, what's yours?" Geoff asked in a gruffly voice.

"It's electroversion, you know, the big improvement from the old fuel cells."

"Oooooo kay, good stuff elek – o - verston."

"Electroversion, electroversion, it's been around for at least twenty years – where have you been?"

"Yes .... uh .... uh," replied Geoff. "Got to go," as he pulled Mike, "other things to do."

They watched as Geoff pulled Mike across the lawn, falling occasionally with Geoff pulling him up. Still pulling on Mike they reached the gate. Mike shouted to the lady, "t-h-a-n-k-s," in a jerky tone.

Mike was stepping into the TS, when the man yelled in a commanding tone, "Hey, ... close the gate."

Mike walked back to the gate, closed it and said, "S-o-r-r-y."

"Miserable S O B," said Geoff as they drove away. After driving nine blocks he turned onto the main road towards the city. The roads were the same, except every few feet there was a light blue strip in the center of the road.

"Wonder what those blue strips are for," said Mike.

"Don't know."

The drive to the city was uneventful. The cars were different in shape, almost a 'round' style and seemed to float on the air rather than touching the road. The TS looked 'out of place'. A driver in an automobile in front of them was reading a newspaper - the car would slow and speed up to the road conditions. Other cars were 'driven' the same way, most people, not paying attention to the driving. Geoff and Mike were taken aback, didn't say anything, looked at each other occasionally, but continued driving.

The city had changed – more buildings, advertising, and the streets were cleaner. Flashy advertising was everywhere, some so high creating distractions – that's what they were actually supposed to do. Many store fronts had continual holographic displays of furniture, home electronic devices and even the food market had displays of how to prepare food.

On Main Street they came to a parking garage. At the entrance a machine popped out a parking permit. A mechanical voice said. "YOUR PARKING SPOT IS 15A ON LEVEL ONE. DO NOT PARK IN ANY OTHER SPOT AS YOUR VEHICLE WILL BE TOWED." The instructions were also being displayed on a screen beside the driver's door. Removing the ticket, the gate opened and they drove to 15A. After parking they walked to the street. Geoff began bumping Mike, in a friendly manner, as they walked.

"In a good mood again," said Mike.

"Always in a good mood," said Geoff.

"Let's look for city hall."

"You ruined it - Ok, but we're only spending fifteen minutes there max. Which way?" asked Geoff.

"Don't know, let's ask somebody."

The people walking didn't pay much attention to them, except the occasional person would smile as they walked by. The clothes people wore all fit perfectly and seemed new – no wrinkles, marks or fading on them.

A young lady walked slowly towards them, smiled, as she was about to pass them.

"'scuse me, maam, can you give me directions to city hall?" asked Mike.

"I don't know exactly where it is, but can check on my locator." She reached into her purse and pulled out a device like a cell phone. She held it in her hand and asked. "Where is city hall?" The device responded, "CITY HALL IS AT 1255 SOUTH MASON STREET. YOU ARE EIGHT BLOCKS SOUTH AND TWO BLOCKS EAST OF CITY HALL. YOU ARE FACING SOUTH, TURN AROUND AND WALK NORTH EIGHT BLOCKS THEN TURN WEST TWO BLOCKS TO 1255 SOUTH MASON STREET."

Mike was amazed at the 'address book'. The lady looked at him, "Haven't you seen a locator before?"

"Uh, Uh, yours looks like a newer model, forgot ours at home," said Mike.

"Thanks got to go," said Geoff as he pulled on Mike.

The lady watched them leave as Geoff had his arm around Mike's shoulder, pulling him.

"Stupid ass," she murmured.

They approached an electronics store; in the window there were holographic displays of products. One 'caught their eye', it was a girl walking on a beach, a small box around her waist, with a hologram projecting an R&R band playing music in front of her.

"Wow, look at that, let's go in."

The store inside was almost 'alive' - holographic images at each display. Three customers in the store were looking at displays and talking to the store clerks. TV sets were three dimensional - their screens projected out in front of a small box. Displays for the TVs stated, "FEEL LIKE YOUR RIGHT AT THE GAME OR PART OF THE CROWD'.

A young man with a goatee was dressed in black pants with a blue 'T' shirt with the store's name on it - 'NOW & GREAT ELECTRONICS STORE INC.' approached them.

"Anything I can help you with - we have the latest IVV units." (FIRST THERE WAS THE VV OR VISUAL VIEWERS

THEN THE IVV OR INTERACTIVE VISUAL VIEWERS. THE NEW NAME FOR TVS.)

"Any questions I can answer for you?"

"Na, just browsing," said Mike.

"Well, if you need information go to the information chair, put on the VR (virtual reality) glasses - the products are demoed there."

He went on to explain that these are the latest IVVs with an adjustable viewing area from a third of a meter to three meters, about the size of this display. (The display had a scale from about 1 to 10 feet). The new IVVs interacted with the viewer to be part of the audience at a game show or even cheering at a sports event. He continued giving them the sales pitch that they have the latest features to interact with – it's a big improvement over the VVs. He turned their attention to the computers in the store. The computers had 46 gigahertz CPUs and 60 tetra byte mole memory drives. They offered a special discount of 15% and at that price they won't last long was. Mike thanked him and said they'd 'look around' and go to the demo area for more information.

"Ok," he said, "remember, when you want to purchase call me," as he walked to another customer.

"Got a computer, Geoff?"

"Na, never had use for one, the only one I used was in school."

"What about the grocery store, don't you use one there?"

"I enter numbers for stock I'm taking to the shelves, don't have to do much 'cause the bar code reader records it."

Mike asked if he ever used the internet – searching for information. Geoff (pointing to his head) said, "my information is up here."

Mike shook his head, 'what a dunce' he thought.

The computers didn't have a physical monitor but displays similar to the VVs. A transparent and floating screen projected, to the front of the computer. There were two 'knobs' on a keypad, one to adjust the screen location – forward or back and the other to make it solid, transparent or anything in between. The computer responded to voice and keyboard commands.

Devices similar to VCRs were on display. A holographic sign with a rotating banner displayed - THE LATEST DVSR RECORDER WITH ONLY A CONTROL BOX THE SIZE OF A SMALL NOTEBOOK. (The DVSR, Digital Video and Sound Recorder, was 6 inches square and about 2 inches high.) The DVSR had indicating lights for – ON and RECORD. All functions were on the remote control, eight buttons in a 'joystick' pattern with a small screen in the upper portion. The screen listed all the functions and how to use them. Recorders didn't use a tape, a card was used to record the video. Displayed above the recorder was 'DSRC CARDS UP TO FOUR HUNDRED AND FIFTY HOURS'. (DSCR - Digital Super Recorder Cards).

Mike was impressed with how the VCRs had changed. Geoff was also and said his VCR can record six hours. With 450 hours, all he'd need is one tape or whatever it was called.

The camcorders were very small, the size of a deck of cards, recording video, and digital pictures. The digital pictures gave a resolution of over 23 mega pixels and up to 2900 pictures per card plus the 8 hours of video.

Another display was a device that you could put on your head to give your health status. It stated that you can give yourself a full medical 'checkup' at home when ever you wanted. They didn't pay much attention to the device, but did notice it.

"Let's get outta' here and find a bookstore."

Mike surprisingly said, "Why a bookstore?"

"Find a book so we can make some money."

"What kind of a book? Like the stock market or sports betting?" asked Mike.

"Ya, that's it," said Geoff.

Geoff asked Mike how much money he had - $63. Geoff had $76. They needed to find a bank to convert the money to 'new' cash – if there was such a thing.

"Is there a bank close to here?" Mike asked a clerk.

"One in the next block, to the left as you leave the store."

They found the bank and went into it expecting to find it the same as in 2004 – it wasn't – there weren't the tellers, just bank vending machines. Only two people behind the counter served the whole bank.

There weren't many customers in the bank. Near the center were the ten vending machines with a man having a 'conversation' with one.

"I'd like three hundred dollars," the man said.

'MONEY CARD OR CASH?'

"Cash"

'PLEASE PLACE YOUR THUMB ON THE PRINT ANALYZER TO COMPLETE THIS TRANSACTION."

In a few seconds a slot opened with fifteen twenties. The man took the money and put it in his wallet.

"WOULD YOU LIKE ANOTHER SERVICE?'

"NO THANKS"

The machine replied in a pleasant tone. "THANK YOU FOR BANKING WITH US."

"We can't use those machines, better talk to someone at the counter," said Mike.

At the counter Mike asked one of the people if they could exchange some older money for some newer cash. He took the money from his wallet and gave it to the lady. She looked at the money and said, "You'll probably get more for these at a money store - collectors will pay a lot more than we will."

"What's a money store?" asked Geoff.

"Where old coins are sold," looking at him with an expression of 'where have you been?'

"Ok," replied Geoff. "Where do we find one?"

"There's one close, go out the door turn left - about three or four blocks down."

"I think it's called MULTINATIONAL COIN AND COLLECTABLES."

They followed the directions to the store. The store inside was not at all like the electronics store. It didn't have any hologram displays. At the counter Geoff told them they had some old money and they'd like to sell it.

"What do you have?"

Geoff handed it to the clerk - one hundred and thirty nine old dollars.

He looked at the money. "These are in very good condition for being a century old."

"How much can we get for them?" Mike asked.

"Let me see, two hundred and eighteen dollars and ninety cents. Where'd you get these?"

"Oh, uh .... uh, found them when cleaning at home," said Mike.

"Must have been there a long time, I'm surprised there's no aging at all."

"You sure you want to sell them?"

"Ya, that's what I said before," said Geoff.

"Do you want cash or a 'Money Card'?"

"Cash," said Geoff in a determined tone.

The clerk counted fives, tens, twenties and three dollars and ninety cents in change. Geoff, put it in his pocket and walked to the door without saying anything.

"Thank you," the clerk said.

"You're welcome," Mike replied.

Mike caught up to Geoff at the door. "Give me my share."

"I'll look after it."

"That's part my money too."

"I'll look after it," Geoff said in a determined tone.

Mike didn't say anything, just walked along with a 'fuming' look on his face. Geoff ignored him.

The paper money was different. Fives were all shades of green and printed on a light green paper. The tens were all shades of green and printed on blue paper. The twenties were all shades of green and printed on an orange paper. On the right bottom of the face side there was a small quarter inch square block - like a flexible computer chip. The chip had scrolling letters on it flashing the denomination.

"Let's get a newspaper and find a burger place," Mike said.

There were newspaper boxes almost at each street corner. The top had a screen and a keypad.

The screen displayed the headline. 'OXYGEN LEVELS IN THE WORLD ARE INCREASING AS THE CARBON DIOXIDE LEVELS DECREASE' and at the bottom of the screen it stated NEWSPAPERS $2.00.

A clear covered tray beside the keypad displayed, 'PLACE MONEY CARD OR $1, $5, $10 OR $20, CHANGE WILL BE RETURNED'. Geoff put $5 on the tray. The top of the box opened with a newspaper and change, Geoff removed it, and the lid closed responding, "THANK YOU."

"A polite newspaper box," said Mike.

Geoff folded the newspaper, didn't say anything, and walked away leaving Mike looking at the screen. He looked up, saw Geoff walking away and ran after him yelling, "wait up."

Geoff snarley said, "I'm looking for a place to eat".

"There's a burger place by the parking garage," said Mike.

"Well, ... let's go get some burgers," said Geoff in an enthusiastic tone.

'BIG BURGER CITY' was next to the parking garage.

It was empty, except for a few teenagers sitting at a table busily talking. They didn't notice Geoff and Mike come in.

Three large boxes, with video screens flashing, 'ORDER HERE', were along the inner wall. They approached the machine, "CAN I TAKE YOUR ORDER."

"Just a minute," replied Geoff, "do you have burgers?"

"PRESS MENU AND THE FOOD WILL BE LISTED. TO VIEW EACH ITEM PRESS 'VIEW' AFTER SELECTING THE ITEM."

They browsed the menu, ordered a cheese burger, cola and large fries by pressing, 'CHEESE BURGERS COMPLETE' then '2' (for two orders) and the view button. A three dimensional rotating image of their order appeared on the screen.

"WHAT CONDIMENTS DO YOU WANT ON YOUR CHEESE BURGER AND WHAT TYPE OF DRINK DO YOU WANT?"

"Ketchup, tomatoes and onions," said Geoff.

'STATE YOUR NAME?'

"Geoff"

"Tomatoes, lettuce and mayo on mine," said Mike.

'STATE YOUR NAME?'

"Mike"

"Wonder why it asked our name," said Mike.

"Don't know."

"YOUR ORDER HAS BEEN ENTERED. PLEASE OPEN THE PAYMENT TRAY AND DEPOSIT TWELVE DOLLARS AND SIXTY CENTS ON IT."

Geoff opened it and placed fifteen dollars on the tray. Closing the tray, the money slid into the machine. The tray returned with change.

'IS THE ORDER 'TO GO' OR WHAT TABLE DO YOU WANT IT DELIVERED TO?'

"How do we select a table?" asked Geoff.

"THE NUMBERS ARE DISPLAYED ON THE FRONT OF EACH TABLE."

Mike was astounded to have all these conversations with machines. Geoff looked around. There were about thirty tables available, table eight was the only one occupied.

"Ok, table one," said Geoff.

"GO TO TABLE ONE AND YOUR ORDER WILL BE DELIVERED IN TWENTY SEVEN SECONDS. THANK YOU GEOFF AND MIKE."

They sat at the table while Geoff looked at the newspaper headline. He then put the newspaper on the table. A door opened at the end of the table, out came two food trays each with small flags and their names on it. The food was on a tray with white colored oval plastic plates, a large restaurant logo was partially hidden under the food.

"Here's to 2104 food," said Mike, as he picked up his burger.

Geoff grabbed his burger and started eating. Mike put some ketchup on his fries. Geoff picked up the ketchup and poured a large amount on his fries. Mike looked at Geoff, how crude he was then picked up his burger. They didn't talk during the meal.

In a few minutes Geoff was done, "that was good." He let out a long low tone 'belch'. "Hurry up, let's get outa' here."

Mike was still finishing his burger, and had a few fries to eat. "I've still got my burger – you eat too fast."

"I eat the way I want to - so get finished."

Mike started eating faster and took a final drink from his glass.

'IS THE FOOD OK AND DO YOU NEED ANYTHING ELSE' - came from the end of the table.

"All done," said Geoff.

"Everything was great," replied Mike.

"IF YOU HAVE COMPLETED YOUR MEAL, PLEASE PRESS THE BUTTON AT THE FRONT OF THE TABLE LABELED 'CLEAN TABLE'."

Mike pressed the button.

"PLEASE REMOVE ALL ITEMS FROM THE TABLE. THEN PRESS THE 'CLEAN' BUTTON."

Mike reached over and pressed the 'clean' button.

'THERE IS A NEWSPAPER ON THE TABLE. PLEASE REMOVE IT FROM THE TABLE AND PRESS THE CLEAN BUTTON.'

Geoff removed the newspaper and set it on an empty chair.

Mike pressed the 'CLEAN' button again.

A door at the end of the table opened and a mechanical hand pulled the trays through the door. Next a wet roller, with a vacuum, cleaned the table spotlessly, and then exited through the same opening. The door closed. They watched this in bewilderment. Mike commented that it was just like a car wash.

"Yea, let's go," said Geoff.

Geoff picked up the newspaper and looked at the front page just to annoy Mike.

"Thought you were in a hurry," Mike said.

"Changed my mind"

Geoff read the headline in a low tone as Mike listened. Industry and cars using less fossil fuels, the amount of carbon dioxide in the air is decreasing, this could cause a cooling of the earth's atmosphere.

"That's different, there was concerned with the cars before," said Mike.

"It says if the levels don't increase, it could cause a reduction of trees and could affect food production in the world – not our problem - won't be here in a hundred years anyway."

Geoff folded the paper abruptly put it under his arm.

"Let's go."

CHAPTER 11

August 5, 2104. Mike and Geoff left the burger place just after half past four. They walked and walked just like tourists, mesmerized by the holographic ads.

Everything imaginable was displayed - vacations, products, movie previews and on and on until they saw books displayed in a store window - novels, travel, business, automobile, computers to name a few.

"Come on Geoff, let's see what kind of books are in here." – Geoff acknowledged.

The automotive section caught Geoff's eye and he went straight there. Mike looked at the signs listing the type of books in each area – computer, technology, self-help, automotive and finally the business section.

Browsing, he saw an interesting one. "FIFTY BEST PERFORMING COMPANIES OVER THE LAST ONE HUNDRED YEARS." Just what he was looking for. It was thin, with a regular book cover, similar to the 2004 books, but when opened, the front page screen displayed 'WELCOME TO THE Fifty BEST PERFORMING COMPANIES OVER THE LAST ONE HUNDRED YEARS'.

The screen changed to instructions:

TO VIEW A PAGE, PRESS 'PAGE BELOW'

TO GO TO MENU PRESS 'MENU'

TO BOOKMARK PAGES PRESS 'BOOKMARK'

TO RETURN TO THE PREVIOUS PAGE PRESS 'PREVIOUS PAGE'

He selected the menu and a list of fifty companies was displayed. His familiarity with the stock market was almost nil, only hearing people made a lot of money. The index contained a section called, 'PERFORMANCE'. Pressing it, a page listing companies ranked as to their performance appeared.

Companies listed, dated to December, 2099. 'INTERNATIONAL ASSOCIATED ADVANCED DEVICES' was listed as number one, touching the name; the company starting date was 2003. Its performance ended in 2099 with the equivalent of $5432 from a meager start of $9.

Geoff was still looking at the automotive books when Mike walked over and showed him. "Look at this!" Mike showed him what he had found and the specific company.

"When did it start to increase?"

"Well, I can find out easy." He pressed 'TREND DETAILS'.

Displayed were details from November 2003 to December 2099. Of particular interest was in October 2003 when it shot up from $28 to $490 in one month.

"Cool," said Mike. "If we put all our money into this stock, we're millionaires in a month."

"Where are we going to get that much cash?"

"Sell your car, our pay, borrow all we can," said Mike.

"What a cool find," said Geoff. "Hold onto that book."

Geoff, still interested in the car book, took 'CAR & TRUCK TEST RESULTS' off the shelf and opened it and a holograph popped up. He ran his finger down the list of 2104 cars and trucks, selecting "SPORT CRUISER – MODEL SC200". A display came alive showing the car, then its performance. A bottom banner displayed, 'IT'S READY FOR THE NEXT PHASE OF ENERFUEL AND THE ADVANCED GUIDANCE SYSTEM'.

It was moving on the road with the driver reading a newspaper while the blue lines guided it. Abruptly it turned onto a road with only lane marking lines.

Across the bottom a banner ....

'ADVANCED GUIDANCE SYSTEM ALLOWS THE DRIVER TO DO OTHER THINGS WHILE THE CAR DRIVES ITSELF. JUST ENTER YOUR START AND END LOCATIONS AND THE CAR DOES ALL THE REST. THE ADVANTAGE IS THE GUIDANCE WILL WORK WITH ALL LINES INCLUDING THE CENTER AND OUTSIDE LANE MARKERS. ONBOARD SENSORS MONITOR AT 360 DEGREES AROUND THE VEHICLE. IT'S THE LATEST AND IT'S ACCIDENT PROOF.'

Displayed next was a safety feature – the car automatically stopped before a washed out bridge. The screen on the car's dashboard displayed, 'BRIDGE INOPERATIVE AHEAD'.

Geoff took both books to a clerk for purchasing.

"Did you find everything you need?" the clerk asked.

"Yea," said Mike. "These are cool books."

"They shouldn't be cool, they are maintained to the temperature of your hand when using them."

"OOO .... kay," said Mike.

The clerk asked if they needed any additional power cells. Geoff thought for a few seconds then said they didn't.

"You can check the power available by turning it over and looking at the power strip," as he showed them where it was.

"Both books have about ninety eight percent power left."

A device read the price of each book and a total displayed was $52.25. Cash or money card the clerk asked.

"Cash," said Geoff.

"Not many people use cash now, a money card is more convenient - soon you won't even need the card when the depth retina system is perfected."

Geoff took his wallet out and gave him the exact amount. The clerk took the money, printed a receipt and put it in the bag with the books. He handed it to Geoff and thanked them for shopping at the store.

"Let's go check City Hall," said Mike.

Geoff looked at a digital clock above the store. "Too late, it's 4:50 - by the time we got there it'll be closed. We'll go back home today and start this investment stuff."

"What's the rush, I still want to find out what happened to my family. Let's look at more stores tomorrow, we'll probably never be back here again – might as well see what's here."

"Ok, we'll find a hotel, go to city hall tomorrow and leave in the afternoon," said Geoff.

They walked until they found a hotel that didn't look expensive and went inside. A woman at the front desk greeted them and asked if they had reservations. Geoff said they didn't, but needed a room for the night.

"What kind of room would you like?"

"Just an ordinary room, TV, uh.................h, oh VV (he remembered), just for tonight."

She asked how many beds they'd needed and Geoff said two.

"That's ninety six dollars."

"Is that the cheapest?" asked Geoff.

"Yes, we're almost full because of the travel convention, that's it - take it or leave it."

Geoff turned to Mike, raised his eyebrows and asked him what he thought. Mike agreed that they should take it because with a convention – how many rooms would be available in other hotels.

Geoff turned to the lady. "We'll take it."

"That will be one hundred and eight dollars and eighty five cents with tax."

"You said it was ninety six dollars - how come it's more?"

"Taxes – do you want it?"

"Guess we're stuck – ye......s," said Geoff.

Geoff gave her cash for the room.

Check out was 3:00 pm tomorrow, your room number is 1, 1, 2, just down the hall to the right - the restaurant is open twenty four hours - cooking machines all twenty four hours - 7:00 am to 9:00 pm there's waitress service.

Whew, she had it all memorized, except for the room number, and added – "one or two keys?"

"Two keys," said Mike.

"Any baggage"

"No, traveling light," said Geoff.

She told them that shaving or other things were available at the vending machines down the hall - you'll pass them on your way to the room – then handed them a key.

The key looked like a large postage stamp (about one inch square). "Place the key on the door's black square, then press the open button."

Geoff carried the newspaper and books as they went to room 112. Mike put the key on the door and pressed the open button. The room was small, a table beside the door, two regular beds and a nightstand between them. Geoff threw the newspaper and the bag on the table.

Mike asked how much cash they had left. Geoff took the money out of his wallet and threw it on the bed then counted it.

"Forty three dollars and twenty cents - we're leaving tomorrow because we're low on cash." He put the money back in his pocket and sat down on the bed.

"Did you notice there aren't any pennies?" said Mike.

"Na, I don't need them – anyway I throw them away."

Geoff missed the question Mike was asking. Everything was rounded to the closest equal five cents so there wasn't any need for pennies.

"How are we going to pay for parking tomorrow?"

"We'll start the time travel from the parking spot."

"Are you sure we can do that - don't we have to be at the Manlee's?"

"We'll drive through the exit to the Manlee's - then we're gone – let them try and find us," Geoff said with a snicker. "Don't worry about it."

"What if an alarm sounds?"

"Let them try and catch us."

"Ok, hope you know what you're doing."

"I do, it's a piece of cake."

Geoff went to the door - he was going to get some shaving supplies and tooth brushes from the vending machine. Mike was still annoyed at Geoff for keeping all the money and not giving him some.

"Ok, I'll turn the TV, uh... VV on."

On the front of the vending machine was a screen with some buttons.

SELECT ALL ITEMS, INSERT A MONEY CARD OR CASH, THEN PRESS OR SAY ACCEPT.

He pressed menu, the machine responded, 'PLEASE SELECT THE ITEMS YOU REQUIRE.'

Not another talking machine he thought. The menu had selection from food to men's needs. He Pressed 'MEN'S NEEDS' and saw the item's they needed -

SHAVING CREAM $2.25

RAZOR AND BLADE $4.00

TOOTH BRUSH $3.00

TOOTHBRUSH AND TOOTHPASTE $5.00

It was expensive he thought. It'll be cheaper if I only get one of each – Mike can use it after me. Grudgingly he pressed shaving cream, razor and blade, toothbrush and toothpaste, then accept.

'ELEVEN DOLLARS AND TWENTY FIVE CENTS' 'PLACE A MONEY CARD OR MONEY ON THE TRAY AT THE BOTTOM.'

Reluctantly he opened the door, placed the exact amount on the tray, closed the door and the money disappeared into the machine.

'Clunk, clung, a pause then a final clunk'. All the items were there, each packaged in plastic bag. He went back to the room carrying all the items.

'Knock .... Knock'

Mike asked who it was.

"It's me, who do you think it is?" Geoff responded in a muffled tone from the outside of the door.

Geoff entered with the vending machine items in his hand. Mike couldn't make out exactly what he had, except for the shaving cream. He asked him if he got everything. Geoff shook his head and threw the bags on the table.

"Yep, expensive, was more than eleven dollars."

Mike saw there was only one of each item and asked where's his razor and tooth brush.

"Too expensive, haven't got much money left – only bought one of each .... you can use them after me."

"I don't want to use your tooth brush." Mike said in a raised tone.

"Tough, you're stuck with it," said Geoff. "I'll use it first then you can use it."

"It doesn't matter anyway we have to use them in the morning again," said Mike.

"No, you don't use it tonight – you use it only in the morning, after me."

"What do I do tonight?"

"I don't know – you're not using the toothbrush until after I'm finished."

Mike, realizing he's not going to persuade his so he dropped the conversation. He looked at the clock in the room – it was 6:00 pm. "Getting hungry?"

"Sort of," said Geoff.

"How much money do we have?"

Geoff was lying on the bed with his hand propping up his head. "Don't know. About thirty three dollars .... let's watch some of this VV, then go eat."

"Let's go now!" pleaded Mike.

"We'll go after the news is over."

The 6:00 pm news started and the picture zoomed to a newsman sitting at a desk.

'VVKAP, CHANNEL 982, SIX O'CLOCK EVENING NEWS'.

The newscaster, Harvey Harrington, as the desk tag stated, started with .... "Today's top headlines are, the moon base was hit by a meteor -- bank robberies are on the rise even with new security measures in place."

He began talking and a video of the moon base came on.

"The moon base was hit by a meteor yesterday. There was damage to one of the elcells supplying power for the station and the breathing air generators. There were a few injuries but none were life threatening. A supply ship left earth base USA-1C for the moon today and is expected to arrive there tomorrow. Sources say they should have it repaired within a week. In the meantime all working activity has been suspended to preserve breathable air. The backup solar collectors are working properly so there's enough electricity to operate the station."

"Now for a commercial break"

The commercial started ....

Two people walking down a street, thunder in the distance.

"DON'T BE CAUGHT WITHOUT A WEATHER PROTECTOR MODEL FOUR. GET THE LATEST, SO SMALL IT WILL FIT IN YOUR POCKET." The commercial showed them holding a small device a few inches square by an inch deep with two buttons and a sliding dial. The buttons were 'ON', 'OFF' and the slider controlled the amount of protection from a small umbrella to a full cover extending to the ground. They turned it on, a transparent umbrella formed over them just as the rain started. The rains bounced off the magnetic umbrella. "THIS IS THE LATEST IN MAGNETIC TECHNOLOGY, THE FORCE FIELDS CAN TOTALLY PROTECT FROM RAIN AND HAIL. THE PROTECTOR FOUR IS ADJUSTABLE FROM SMALL SHIELDING TO FULL COVERAGE. DON'T GET CAUGHT IN THE RAIN OR HAIL WITHOUT ONE."

"That's quite an umbrella, did you see that?" asked Mike.

"Ya, should take one back – could make some money selling it."

"We don't have enough money," said Mike. "Have to eat tonight, that'll probably drain us of a lot of cash."

Harvey returned to the screen, starting the next story.

"Bank robberies have been on the increase for the past three months. Sophisticated bank robbers using military type weapons and force field protection shields are breaking security technology. A robbery this afternoon was recorded by one of our news crews. Jane Wilson has the story."

"Hello, I'm Jane Wilson, robberies are on the increase and military type equipment is being used as you can see from what happened this afternoon."

The scene switched to three people coming out of a bank, guns drawn and having duffle bags over their shoulders. Police cars surrounded the front of the bank.

The police uniforms were different, skin tight, but very flexible.

Jane commented the protective force field armor used by the robbers was the older type but still capable of stopping any type of gunfire including the static ray shots. From inside the force field they can return any type of fire. "This is a big disadvantage for the police."

An officer spoke over an amplified speaker.

"This is the police, lay down your weapons, you will not be harmed."

The bank robbers responded with gunshots, not like bullets but green rays of light. The police ducked behind the car doors, getting bombarded with rays, burning holes in the metal. The police fired their guns. Blue rays, hit the force field and bounced vertically up.

"There's a helicopter hovering above .... over the roof. The magnetic field will collapse when they drop the metallic particles," commented Jane.

Maneuvering into place was difficult. Shots were fired at the helicopter, missing it by inches. It moved into the proper position quickly and dropped the metal particles then pulled back over the roof. The particles fell to the force fields, violent sparks erupted, the shields collapsed.

The robbers kept firing. Gunfire was returned by the police. A police officer, gun in hand, reached over the roof of a police car and fired. A red wave spread, like a tidal wave, in the direction of the robbers. Stunned, they dropped to the ground. The police rushed them and put something like a collar around the robber's necks. "The police have put the calming ropes around their necks disabling them." (Calming ropes sedated electronically, making the person calm and agreeable, generally eliminating the need for handcuffs.)

"It's fortunate they didn't have the new military shields, they're not affected by the metal particles."

"This is Jane Wilson for VVKAP news, back to you Harvey."

The picture switched to the station, Harvey continued. "Thanks Jane, that was some incredible footage - we'll be back after a commercial break."

"Did you see that?" Mike asked.

"Yea, that's sure cool stuff."

"Ready to eat," said Mike.

"Guess it's time," replied Geoff, as he turned off the VV. "We'll go back to the burger place .... the hotel is probably too pricey."

At the check in counter, the clerk looked at them walking by. "Enjoying your stay with us - let me know if we can do anything more for you."

"Yea," said Geoff.

He turned to Mike, "what kind of remark is that - probably cost us to do 'anything more'."

Knowing the direction to the burger place, they got there in a few minutes. It was crowded, only table 12 open. Mike sat at the table while Geoff was ordering.

'YOU CANNOT SIT AT THE TABLE UNLESS YOU ORDER A MEAL."

Mike replied, "We're ordering, we're ordering - give us a few minutes."

'You HAVE 5 MINUTES TO ORDER AND THEN THIS TABLE WILL BE SHUT DOWN. YOU SHOULD ORDER AND SELECT THE TABLE BEFORE YOU SIT HERE.'

"What do you mean 'shut down'," said Mike.

'THE TABLE AND CHAIRS WILL BE ROLLED UP. NO ONE WILL BE ABLE TO SIT AT THE TABLE UNTIL AN ORDER IS PLACED AND THIS TABLE IS SELECTED.'

"Strange, having a conversation with a table," Mike said.

He shouted at Geoff. "Hurry up or the table will shut down."

People at the other tables stared at Mike.

Geoff turned, "ok, ok, do you want the same as this afternoon?"

"Yea", responded Mike, "just order and select table twelve."

"What table?"

"Twelve," Mike yelled. Some people looked, and then went back to eating.

"All done" Geoff walked to the table and sat across from Mike. "One minute, thirty four seconds."

"That's longer than this afternoon," said Mike.

The order was delivered the same as before. They ate and left.

"Sure gets annoyed if you don't order before you sit," said Mike.

The sky was dark, but the streets were lit by 'old fashioned' pole lights.

"Let's get back to the hotel and watch some TV uh .... VV – can't get used to that," said Mike.

Back at their room, they turned on the VV.

'THE TIME TRAVELERS IN SPACE' was just starting to play on the VV.

"Wonder when this was made?" said Mike.

"How can I know that?" said Geoff.

"Sorry, didn't mean for you to tell me, looks new."

"Look in the paper, there's probably a VV guide."

Mike picked up the paper, flipped through it finding a column - 'TODAY'S VV GUIDE'. The movie was made in 2098.

At 11 pm, after the movie was over, Geoff went into the bathroom taking the toothbrush and toothpaste. A few minutes later he came out and put the toothbrush on the nightstand. He told Mike that he could use it in the morning after he was finished. Mike went to the bathroom. He spent some additional time gurgling and spitting – just to try to annoy Geoff. Didn't work - when he returned from the bathroom Geoff was sleeping. Mike turned out the light, gave a sigh of relief, and went to sleep. Both slept well, but the excitement would begin tomorrow.

CHAPTER 12

August 28, 2004. It was early in the morning. Chris didn't go into the house. He didn't want to wake Jennifer and tell her what happened - yet. He did sleep some, about 4 hours, with his head on the table and his arms as the 'pillow'. He woke at after 5:30 am, not really rested, and began working on the time traveling device.

Jennifer woke just before 8:00 am. Chris wasn't in bed and his side of the bed didn't look slept in. She got dressed and went to the TS building. For a minute she stood there shocked, the TS was gone and Chris was working on the portable time travel devices. He had a small square bandage on the back of his head.

Jennifer in a concerned tone asked ....

"What happened to your head? Where's the TS?"

"Whoooo,........................ I'll explain.

Last night, just before midnight, the same two men who broke in a few days ago came back."

"What happened to the back of your head?" she questioned.

Chris explained that he was looking at the sketches and notes when he was attacked from behind, got knocked over and in the process hit his head on the table. When he regained consciousness, the TS began to disappear and the computer recorded the date as August 5, 2104, but the time was missing.

"Are you sure you're ok, shouldn't you see a doctor?" she asked in a concerned tone.

"It's a little sore, I'll survive."

"What can we do to get the TS back from those hoodlums," she said.

"I'm going to finish one of the portable devices, and go after the TS," Chris said.

"Finish two of them, I'm going with you!"

Chris was concerned, the time travel devices had never been tested (as far as he knew) but the operation was nearly the same as the TS.

Jennifer was determined and repeated that she was going too - so make them both functional.

When Chris had traveled in the TS he had experienced weather changes, sometimes severe. He suggested Jennifer go to the city to see what she could find in the way of a weather protection type of suit at a sporting goods store.

She drove to the city and thought a military surplus or sky diving store at the airport might have something they could use. A military store on Crane Street might have them, if they didn't have anything, she'd try a sky diving place, at the airport.

The military store carried surplus military items from all over the world, even specialty items such as full coverage suits with helmets. Entering the store she saw a display close to the purchase counter. She spotted something they could use - two full coverage suits with helmets, but with no price tag. Three clerks were in the store. Two far down an isle with other customers. The third clerk, a girl, at the cash register, didn't seem to be interested in what Jennifer was looking at and was reading a magazine.

"How much are those suits," she asked – no answer.

"Excuse me, how much are those suits," she said in a louder voice.

The girl looked up and said, "what was that?"

"The suits you have on the stand, how much are they and what were they used for."

"Un, oh, those are military suits with full thermal insulation, interlocking helmets and weatherproof - some people buy them for sky diving."

"What about boots?"

"You can use anything, even shoes as the suit comes down and covers your feet."

"How much are they?"

"Well, they're in very good condition, no rips," she paused, thought for a few seconds. "Had them for a while, I'll sell them for three hundred a piece."

"What size are they?"

"They're adjustable for any normal size person, sort of a 'one size fits all'."

"That's fine, I'll take both of them," said Jennifer.

At home she showed them to Chris.

"I think these will work, they're full protection with thermal insulation, weatherproof and a full interlocking helmet. The girl in the store said some people used them for sky diving."

"Looks great, just what we need," replied Chris. "We're going to need money they use in 2104." His idea was to buy some gold coins and sell them in 2104 to get the current money. "I'd think in a hundred years the money would be different."

They discussed how many they'd need and 10 was the amount. They didn't know what they'd be worth in the future – possibly four or five hundred each.

"Ok! I'll get them, you keep working on the time travel devices."

"Got one done and I'm getting close on the other – should have it done later today."

She drove to the bank and asked the teller if they had gold coins. The teller said they didn't have any but could order them – be here in a few days or you can go to a coin store.

"There's one about four blocks from here - I think it's called Multinational Coin or something like that. Go out the door and turn left, you can't miss it."

Jennifer left the bank, followed the directions and in four blocks saw a sign - 'MULTINATIONAL COIN AND COLLECTABLES'.

The store wasn't busy. She walked up to the counter and inquired. The clerk asked her what kind – US Eagles, Maple Leafs, Kangaroo or Krugerrand.

"How much are they, the one ounce pure gold ones?"

"They're all the same gold content – one troy ounce and same price."

"Ok, I'll take ten of the US Eagles."

He went behind the counter, opened a book and looked on a list. "That will be four thousand one hundred and seventy dollars for ten."

"Can you take a check?"

"Yes, but we can't release the coins until the check clears. We take credit cards and you can have the coins right away."

"Fine, I'll use my credit card then."

Jennifer gave him her credit card. The clerk ran the card through the reader and waited for purchase approval. In a few seconds an approval slip was printed.

"Just sign here and the coins are yours."

She signed the slip.

"Go to the back with this receipt and they'll give you the coins."

She passed the receipt through a slot at the bottom of the window.

The man inside the protected area looked at the receipt, went to a bin and counted out ten coins. He filled out another receipt for 10, one troy ounce gold eagle coins.

"Please sign the bottom line and slide it back through the slot."

She signed it and along with the pen slid it in the slot. "Do you want the coins in a bag?"

"Yes that would be fine."

He put the receipts and coins in a small plastic bag, passed them through the slot in the window, with a "thank you."

Jennifer acknowledged and drove home.

"Get the coins?"

"I got ten," said Jennifer "We'll split them up in case we get separated."

"Good idea"

"How are the time devices coming?"

"Very close to being done."

"We should take a small flashlight with us – we might need one."

"Yes, it'll be dark when we get there."

Chris retained nearly all the components his father had used in the time traveling devices including the older CPUs. He changed the Ram memory to flash memory for better reliability. Both time traveling units were ready for a power supply and module testing. In a couple of hours the testing was complete. The old CPUs were the cause of the heating problem limiting the time travel his father had written in the letter. Perhaps if he used the newer CPUs and memory, less heat would be generated. He thought he would modify the devices when he got back - a hundred years shouldn't be a problem.

"Are you sure it'll be ok?" Jennifer questioned.

"From the way dad designed and built it I can't see any problems at all for a short time travel distance."

"Ok, don't forget to take the spare keys for the TS, I've got the flashlight."

"Got them," he picked the keys up and put them in his pocket.

It was 6:20 pm; they put on the protective suits and the time devices. They turned them 'ON'. Using the knobs, they set the top indicator to August 5, 2104, arriving at 9 pm, to get there at night so they wouldn't be noticed when they materialized.

They did a final date check. Chris read the date and Jennifer acknowledged by reading it back. About ten feet from the TS area, close to the computers, they held hands and did a countdown.

Chris started counting ....

5, 4, 3, 2, and on 1, they pressed their 'START T TRIP' button gradually fading from 2004.

The units didn't give off any glow or sounds like the TS. Without a boost voltage the time sequence was slow. As they traveled, the TS building was deteriorating, vegetation was changing with the seasons, night and day was changing rapidly along with the weather. The suits worked well, protecting them through all the momentary weather changes. They experienced a sensation like 'floating on air'. Just moments into the trip, around 2056, they lost their handgrips and lost sight of each other. Jennifer arrived first and looked to find Chris. He should have been beside her. A few minutes later he materialized beside her. No lights or sounds as they materialized in 2104.

"What happened, I was getting worried?" asked Jennifer.

"Had a problem with this unit, it kept slowing down then speeding up, that's when we lost our hand grip - I'll have to fix the problem when we get back."

Jennifer unzipped the side of her suit and took the flashlight out of her pocket. She handed it to Chris.

"It's chilly here," she said. Zipping her suit up quickly.

"Let's go in the house and see where we can sleep tonight."

The TS building had almost collapsed and the whole area appeared abandoned. Chris shone the flashlight around the building and on the road. There were fresh tire tracks leaving the building, going over the roll up door and leading out to the main road.

"Guess they were here, there's tracks leading to the road," said Chris.

They turned around and looked at the house. It was spooky for a cool, clear night. For what they could see with the flashlight, the house looked eerie, badly in needed of repairs.

The front door was unlocked, creaked when they opened it. Many windows were broken.

"Spooky!" said Jennifer.

"It'll have to do for tonight," said Chris.

The flashlight lit up the main level bedroom, the one where he had his computer, there was a bed, with a dusty mattress on it. An old dusty blanket was lying on the floor.

They turned over the mattress; it was cleaner on the other side. They shook out the blanket. They removed their helmets, shoes and travel devices and placed them beside the bed. They laid the blanket over the bed. Chris was asleep in a few minutes being tired from the night before. Jennifer lay awake for a longer time, but eventually fell asleep.

CHAPTER 13

August 6, 2104. It was just after 6 in the morning and the sun started to peek over the horizon - its rays coming through a front broken window and gradually to the bedroom where Chris and Jennifer were sleeping. Chris slept soundly all night, but Jennifer hadn't. The sunlight was like a wake up call. It eventually shone on Jennifer's face, she moved her hand to shade her face and rolled her eyes to see where they were, unbelieving, in the future.

"Are you awake?" she asked.

"Um, Um, yes, slept reasonably well last night, how about you?"

"Not too good, this mattress was sure uncomfortable – I'll put the coffee on," she said in a joking manner. "Better get up and get going so we can get things back to normal," she said sitting up.

Chris opened his eyes, gave a yawn then sat up.

"These suits aren't the most comfortable thing to sleep in," said Chris.

"What are we going to do with the suits and time devices?"

"We'll put them behind the loose boards at the rear the stairs, they'll be safe there 'til we come back for them."

Jennifer agreed and walked into the kitchen. The table was covered with a thin layer of dust. She stood and looked around the kitchen - it was very depressing – looking at the condition of their home which they had taken such good care of – although they were a hundred years in the future.

Two chairs, with partially broken backs, were facing the sink. She walked over and looked out the window above the sink, it was one of the few windows still unbroken. The sink was stained and chipped. She tried to turn on the water tap with no luck. She looked in the cupboard, the high one above the sink's window. Opening the door - it creaked. It was empty, closing it, some dust fell down. She opened the door to the left of the sink, inside were some cups and plates, dusty, but still intact. Opening the cupboard to the right of the sink she was surprised to see a coffee maker, dusty, but looked like it would still work. The glass pot was broken at the top but the handle was still intact.

"We have a coffee pot but no coffee," she said jokingly.

Chris came into the kitchen. He looked out the window towards the crumbling TS building and could see the fruit trees. Some of the trees had fruit, but much of the fruit had fallen to the ground. The grass had grown wild, being neglected for a very long time.

"At least we can have some fruit for breakfast," Chris said as he turned to her.

"Ok, guess that's better than nothing," she said.

They walked out the door and through the remains of the TS building where Chris noticed a pot lying on the floor with water in it. They'd be able to wash at least. The water was clear, but had dust particles floating on it. In the orchard they picked some fruit and walked back to the house. Chris was carrying the fruit so Jennifer picked up the water and brought it to the house. "Sure could still use a cup of coffee," said Jennifer as she started to eat an apple.

"I could too," as he started to eat one.

"We'll have to get to the city, track down the location of the TS and get some breakfast."

"Got to exchange some money first for the coins, need to find a bank or coin store," replied Jennifer.

He needed to check if the TS was in the area. He removed the tracking receiver from his pocket, turned it on and got a weak signal pointing towards the city.

"They're still here," he said, "we'd better find it before they go back."

After finishing the fruit and cleaning up a bit they removed the suits. Their regular clothing was underneath, but a little wrinkled.

Gathering the suits and travel devices they took them to the basement and placed them behind the loose boards.

"Now, how are we going to get to the city," Jennifer said.

Chris held his hand up with his thumb out. "This way"

"Ok, let's do it," said Jennifer as they walked down the broken driveway to the main road.

The city had expanded almost to their property. Pulling out the TS locator at the main road, Chris turned it on and pointed it to the city. It had a stronger signal, so the TS was well within the range of the locator.

They waited only a few minutes for a car to come along. Chris flagged the car with his hand, it stopped beside them and the passenger side window rolled down. A young woman, in her twenties, was driving and reading a magazine at the same time. She raised her head and looked at them.

"Can we get a ride to the city?" he asked.

"How far ya going?"

"Any place in the city will do," said Jennifer.

"Just going to the bank on Crane Street - can give you a ride to there," the woman replied.

"That's perfect," replied Chris.

Jennifer got in the back and Chris in the front passenger side.

The car was almost round on the inside, with four bucket seats.

She pressed resume, the car proceeded and she started to talk.

"You're lucky I looked up - I was reading and not paying attention."

Chris and Jennifer looked at each other with a puzzled look – who's driving?

The woman asked where they were from. Jennifer replied that they used to live at the Manlee's place a while ago, but were vacationing in the area.

"Don't think you'll find anyone there now - the property hasn't been lived in for almost sixty years. Someone was supposed to be there back in the thirties, but left during the drought in the forties," she said. "Although, I don't know it's just rumors – some people say it's haunted because there's strange lights there every once in a while and tire marks go into the garage and disappear."

"Oh, we were here for a brief period in the early nineties." said Jennifer quickly, "but we left because there was too much work to get it livable."

"That's interesting", said the girl, "the reason some people say it's haunted was 'cause there were two people who lived there about a century ago and disappeared."

Chris looked at Jennifer and commented that he hadn't heard that one.

"I was there at night a few years ago - didn't see any ghosts though," she said. "The other rumor is they got into a time machine, disappeared and never came back - don't know 'though it was way before my time."

Chris looked at Jennifer again and thought, 'Hope this doesn't mean we didn't get back.'

"Come to think of it, the people who lived there had a brother who took over the property and kept it up until the fifties - someone called Rich Manlee owns it now."

Chris turned to Jennifer and in a low tone said, "must be Rich's grand son."

She had been talking to them the whole time and didn't have her hands on the steering wheel but the car would speed up and slow down for different driving conditions even stopping at a 'STOP' sign."

"How is this car driven?" asked Chris.

"Just have to enter the start and end points – its got the old type of guidance that still goes by the light blue lines - would like to get a newer car that uses the center and outside lines," she explained.

"Oh," replied Chris as Jennifer gave him a nudge and shook her head 'No'.

"Just wondering if it had the newer system," Chris said trying to get out of this one.

They were reaching the city; she switched it to manual mode and started to drive the car. In a few minutes they arrived at the bank where she stopped next to a parallel parking spot. She pressed a 'Park' button and the car move sideways into the parking spot.

"That's technology," said Chris.

The girl looked at him in a strange way almost saying 'where have you been', but didn't.

"Thanks for the ride," said Jennifer.

"An interesting conversation," said Chris.

"You're welcome."

She pressed a button and all the doors opened.

It was cloudy and a little rain began to fall, almost like a mist. The woman opened her purse and pulled out a small device, pressed 'ON' then with a sliding control adjusted the umbrella just above her head.

"What's that thing?" asked Chris.

"It's a magnetic umbrella," she said. "This model came out a few weeks ago – it's much smaller than the older model."

"Where can we get one?" asked Jennifer.

"Just about any store - have to go, I have to get to the bank."

"This looks sort of familiar," said Jennifer, "should be near the place I got the coins before we left."

"If we go down this way a few blocks, we should reach the coin store if it's still there." Above the buildings they could see the holographic advertising displays and the active store windows.

They walked down the street and there it was "MULTINATIONAL COIN AND COLLECTABLES"

"That's where I got the coins before we left. I'm surprised it's still here. Let's see what we can get for them now."

They walked into the store and up to the counter. A clerk was standing there and looked up when they approached.

"Can we change some gold coins for cash," said Jennifer.

"Sure, what do you have?" asked the clerk.

"Five US Eagles," she said.

Handing the coins to the clerk, "what are they worth?"

He looked at them for a few seconds, shifted them from back to front.

"They look in very good condition and over a hundred years old. They're worth ---," as he looked it up, "eight hundred and twenty dollars and ninety cents each."

"That sounds good," Chris said.

"If you were here yesterday, you'd have gotten about two dollars more for them."

"I can give you cash or a money card."

"What's a money card?" said Jennifer.

He looked at her a little strange. "It's as good as cash - you can use it anyplace and if you want any money you can go to the bank and get cash with it."

"A money card is fine," said Jennifer.

"Must be a run on money that's over a hundred years old. There were two guys in here yesterday that had money from the early two thousands, it looked almost new."

"We're looking for them - do you know where they went or their names?" asked Chris eagerly.

"No, didn't get their names it was a cash sale."

"Which way did they go?" asked Jennifer.

"Just walked out the door - think they turned left."

"Well that's four thousand one hundred and four dollars and fifty cents on the money card - sign here for the card and it's all yours after we get a thumb print on it."

He moved a small machine to the center of the counter. It had a green shiny surface with four areas marked with white lines around two inches squares numbered 1, 2, 3 and 4. Pressing a button marked 'Clean', the green area turned red then back to green - after a few seconds flashed 'READY'. "Do both of you want to have access to the card - can be used by up to four people."

"Yes," said Jennifer.

"Ok, one of you put your right thumb on 'one'."

Jennifer put her thumb on the square marked 'one' and almost instantly displayed 'NEXT OR COMPLETED'. Jennifer removed her thumb and he told Chris to do the same thing but on square number 'two'. Chris followed his directions, removed his thumb from the machine. The clerk pressed the "COMPLETED' BUTTON and out the side came a card just slightly smaller than a credit card. It looked like a normal credit card without their names on it, just a 12-digit number with five strange Greek looking symbols after the numbers. On the top of it was 'CARD AREA 17 MONEY CARD."

"All done," and he handed her the card. She thanked him and he said to come and see them again.

Leaving the store Chris said, "Well they were here yesterday and they didn't go back yet, the TS should be close – better start looking for it right now."

Chris took the tracker out of his pocket and turned it on. It pointed north. Hastily they walked until it pointed to a parking garage. Going inside the garage the tracker pointed to the area in the direction of 15A.

"There it is," Jennifer said. They looked around and couldn't see anyone so they walked up the ramp.

Chris decided to disabled it until they could decide how to bring them back. He got the keys out of his pocket pressed 'unlock' and opened the back door. Reaching to the control module he removed a small card about the size of a credit card and put it in his pocket. That disabled the control module so they couldn't time travel.

"What about them driving out of here – we'd have to go find it again – shouldn't we disable the ignition?" asked Jennifer.

"Good idea," he closed the back and went to the front door and pulled the 'hood' handle. He opened the hood, and in the relay box he removed the relay marked 'Start Relay' then replaced the cover and closed the hood.

"That'll keep them from going anyplace until we get back" as he put the relay into his pocket. "Let's get something to eat."

"Ok,' said Jennifer. "I'd like to look around and see what's here - don't know if we'll be back again."

"You remember the umbrella the girl had - we should get a couple of them," said Chris "might be able to use them instead of the travel suits."

"Would be a lot easier"

"We'd better be careful, I sure don't want those guys to see us."

The TS was disabled. It was time to get something to eat, do some site seeing and shopping, Maybe?????????

CHAPTER 14

August 6, 2104. It was already mid morning. Holographic billboards were everywhere, even the storefronts had similar types of displays. They walked down the street, almost mesmerized, looking at the displays and watching for a restaurant. The advertising and the spectacular displays in the stores kept them from noticing the restaurants - they had walked by a few.

Jennifer was thrilled about a soda pop hologram that extended high from a building. It was a person handing a cup to anyone but extended to street level. A person standing in the right spot appeared to have it handed to them. The display caption read 'SODA POP SO GOOD YOU CAN DRINK IT ALL THE TIME - IT'S EVEN HEALTHY'.

"It feels like we're actually in the display," she said.

"Yes, and it looks like their done with lasers," said Chris.

"Look over there," as he pointed to a place high on one of the buildings, "the lasers are coming out of boxes on the building corners."

The advertising didn't affect any of the people walking by – they just ignored them. Chris was still looking at the hologram; Jennifer looked at the storefronts and saw a restaurant - 'Shannon's Café'.

"Want some breakfast," said Jennifer, "that restaurant looks small and cozy – let's try it?"

Chris looked at the restaurant and agreed. It was busy, but still a few tables empty that needed cleaning. A friendly lady wearing a nametag 'SHANNON' greeted them. "Would you like breakfast?"

"Yes, for two," replied Chris.

"It will only be a few minutes," as she went over to a table at the back of the café and signaled a waitress to come over, take the dishes away and wipe the table. Coming back to Chris and Jennifer she said, "please follow me the table is ready."

After being seated she said, "someone will be here shortly to set the table."

A waitress came to the table and set the cutlery. "Would you like coffee?"

"Yes," Jennifer said in a definite tone.

"Black, with natural cream, art cream, sweet cream, real sugar, sweetener all, sweetener sum or sweet and creamy natural," she said.

"Uh .... uh, just coffee with natural cream and real sugar," replied Jennifer.

"Ok" she replied and went over to the counter and asked for two coffees, both nc and ns. A girl behind the counter poured the coffee, set them on a tray with a bowl of sugar and a pitcher of cream. The waitress took the tray and set the coffees, cream and sugar on the table. They mixed the cream and sugar into their coffee, took a sip.

"Do you have menus?" Jennifer asked.

"Press 'menu' on the screen."

Jennifer pressed 'MENU'; it next displayed "PRESS THE DESIRED 'MEAL' YOU WOULD LIKE TO VIEW, 'BREAKFAST – LUNCH – DINNER'. She pressed 'BREAKFAST' and the display changed to a list of breakfast items.

"There's quite a selection of items," said Jennifer. "Haven't heard of many of these things – what are paneggs and eggbatoppers?"

"Don't know, but I'm going to have the standard two eggs, bacon, potatoes with an Orange juice," said Chris as he sipped his coffee.

"I'll order the same except with Apple juice."

The waitress came over and said, "Ready to order?"

"Yes," said Jennifer. "We'll both have the two eggs, bacon and potatoes with a juice, Orange for Chris, Apple for me."

"How would you like your eggs?"

"Scrambled," said Jennifer.

She asked if they'd like toast and gave a selection of brown, white, black, seeded, rye, sourdough or full grains. They both said sourdough.

"If you want ketchup or sauces press 'sauces' on the screen."

Chris pressed the 'sauces' button, the door opened at the end of the table with ketchup and a selection of five other sauces.

"Haven't heard of any of these - Zuke sauce - wonder what it is?" said Chris.

"I'll have ketchup," said Jennifer. "I'm not brave enough to try anything new."

Their coffee was nearly finished when the waitress brought the coffee pot over. "More coffee?"

"Yes," they replied and she poured the coffee.

In ten minutes she brought them their orders.

"If you need anything else just press service on the display menu."

"Ok," responded Chris.

After they finished Chris pressed 'service', the waitress came to the table. They asked for their check. The waitress said to press 'final bill' on the screen and it will display the cost. He pressed 'FINAL BILL' and displayed was a total of twenty eight dollars and seventy cents. The top of the screen displayed 'MONEY CARD OR CASH. IF MONEY CARD, PLACE THE CARD IN THE ACCEPT SLOT BELOW AND YOUR RIGHT THUMB ON THE AREA LABELED ID. WITH THE MONEYCARD IF YOU WANT TO LEAVE A TIP, SAY THE AMOUNT. IF CASH, TAKE THE BILL TO THE CASHIER.'

"Four dollars and fifty cents"

The machine responded, 'THANK YOU. PLEASE SAY 'COMPLETE' TO ACCEPT THE TOTAL OF THIRTY-THREE DOLLARS AND TWENTY CENTS. PLEASE INSERT MONEY CARD.'

Jennifer got the money card from her pocket, placed it in the slot, placed her thumb on the proper place and said "Complete".

In a few seconds the machine responded 'DO YOU WANT A PRINTED RECEIPT?'

"No," said Jennifer.

She took the money card from the slot and put it in her pocket. Turning to Chris she said, "shall we go." They walked out to the street and resumed looking at the store windows. A store that caught Jennifer's eye displayed women's clothing. The window had clothes being modeled by hologram models. The display changed every few minutes to a new design.

"Let's go in," she said.

"Ok, only for a few minutes - we have to find the guys who stole the TS and bring them back."

They walked into the store and were inundated by the displays. Jennifer looked from one end to the other. Many areas had hologram models in mid air modeling the clothes in that section. One attractive display was the designer jeans.

"I do need some new jeans – these are interesting." It was a girl walking, then stopping and changing the style and color of her jeans on the spot.

Looking at the jeans bin, they were all one size, blue and stated 'FORM FITTING AT THE TOUCH'. A flap pulled out of the left front pocket with a push button pad.

The display above the jeans stated what the pad could do.

FITTING – LOOSE, NORMAL, TIGHT

COLOR – DARK BLUE, LIGHT BLUE, RED, BLACK

SELECT AFTER YOU HAVE PUT THE GARMENT ON.

"Chris, I'm going to try one on."

A clerk noticed them and began to walk over. She was in her twenties with dark brown hair. The hair was done in a strange way, the front was long and as it went back it was very short, about a half inch. She had a shiny top that changed patterns, almost like a kaleidoscope. Her pants changed from black to grey to dark red as she walked. For every step, the colors would flow slowly around the pants.

"Look at those pants and top," said Jennifer.

"Quite an outfit," said Chris, just as she walked up to them.

"Can I help you?"

"Yes, I'd like to try on these jeans," Jennifer said.

"The fitting rooms are in the corner - just press the button and the door to an unoccupied one will open."

Jennifer, carrying the pants, pressed the button and a door opened. In the dressing room, she put on the jeans and came out. They were very baggy and too long.

"Use the selector for color and fitting – the pad is in the left pocket."

Jennifer flipped the pad out of the left pocket, pressed 'ON', then pressed normal and light blue.

In a few seconds the jeans were a normal fit, proper length and changed from dark blue to light blue starting at the waist, down to bottom of the legs.

"Wow," she said. "This is fantastic - I'll take these."

"They are the latest design – just came out a week ago."

"How much are they?"

"One hundred and ten dollars, take them to the 'check outer' (a machine that replaced a clerk) and you can pay there."

"Ok!"

"Can I wear them?"

"Yes, then I'll have to do it manually - do you want to pay with a money card or cash?"

"Money card," said Jennifer.

"Ok, come to the front and I'll deactivate the antitheft sensor."

"Just a minute, I have to go get my things out of the dressing room."

Jennifer got her old jeans, went to the manual checkout and handed her the money card.

"Don't see many of those types of jeans anymore," said the clerk as she used a hand device to scan over the jeans Jennifer was wearing.

The device gave a 'ping' sound. "The jeans are clear now."

Chris noticed a display for the magnetic umbrellas.

"We'd like two of these," he said as he got two from the display and handed them to her.

"Yes" said the clerk. "These are the new ones – Weather Protector Model Four and can actually cover you totally even keeping out hail .... compared to the Model three, they're better and pocket size."

"Do they need flashlight batteries?" asked Chris.

The clerk looked at him in a strange way and said, "We haven't used those batteries in many years, that's even before my time. These are powered by enercells, the mini fuel cells."

"Ok" said Chris and continued, "Where can we get some spare enercells?"

"These cells will last at least five years under normal use, and you can refill them when that happens."

"Ok, we'll take the two umbrellas, how much are they?"

"Forty dollars each"

"Put them on the money card also," said Chris.

She took a hand scanner pointed it at the jeans Jennifer had on and at the two umbrellas. None of the items had bar codes. She looked at a screen on the counter.

"That will be one hundred and ninety dollars - put your right thumb here."

Jennifer did and soon a receipt was printed.

The girl put the old jeans and the magnetic umbrellas in a bag, said, "thank you, come again."

"Have to come back when we have more time."

"Does that mean you'll do some more time traveling?"

She just smiled at him. Above they could see a large digital clock on a building. It was ten minutes past noon.

CHAPTER 15

August 6, 2104. It was early afternoon and Geoff and Mike had checked out of the hotel. They walked to the TS to put the books in it. Geoff had the remote control, pressed the unlock button, the lights flashed and there was a series of 'clicks' unlocking the doors. The TS looked normal, no reason to suspect some vital parts were removed.

"Everything ok," said Mike.

"Ya," said Geoff. "We should get back and start investing - make some cash."

Mike still wanted to find out about his family. Geoff hesitatingly said yes and said he didn't want to spend a lot of time at city hall. He wanted to go back home this afternoon.

"All we do is press a button and move the switch - don't think they'd make it complicated - anyway, we'll see what's to be done after getting back from the hall," said Mike.

Geoff put the books behind the front seat and pressed 'lock' on the remote control. 'Beep, beep' and the lights flashed twice. Geoff told him he had an hour, then they were gone. Mike asked him why he wasn't interested in his own family. He didn't respond as they left the parking garage and headed to city hall. Geoff looked at the big digital clock, it was 12:32 pm. "You have an hour - 'til 1:30 - do you know how to get there?"

"Yea, it's just down here a ways," said Mike.

They bumped each other, as they walked to the city hall becoming very noticeable and catching the attention of Chris and Jennifer, walking on the other side of the street. Chris pointed to them and told Jennifer that they were the two that stole the TS. He pulled Jennifer gently into a convenience store. They watched through a window until Geoff and Mike were out of view - blocked by the cars and the people on the street.

"What'll we do?" asked Jennifer.

"At least we know they're not at the TS, we've time to do something."

They continued on their way to city hall not expecting Chris and Jennifer had watched them. A few blocks before city hall Mike and Geoff passed a sporting goods store. A hologram in the window showed a man fishing, catching one with almost every cast. Along the bottom a banner read 'USE THE LATEST PROGRAMMABLE ELECTRONIC FISHING LURE - IT ACTS LIKE A REAL FISH'.

"What a lure," said Mike, "wana' go inside?"

"No, your time's a tickin'."

A few blocks later, they reached city hall. It was an older building, but with modern (2104) features. It was four stories high taking up a full city block. The lawn had flowers along a walkway to the main double doors. There were four glass elevators on each of the corners of the building. Geoff and Mike ignored the appearance of the building and entered through the main door. In the building was a big lobby with 'current' statues. Straight ahead were escalators, but without steps. To the right in front of them was a four-foot square screen displaying departments and directions to each. Beside each department there was a number stating 'PEOPLE WAITING TO BE SERVED'.

At the screen Mike looked at the list, then came to:

CITY HALL RECORDS – MAIN FLOOR ROOM 102 - PEOPLE WAITING TO BE SERVED '0'.

"Ok, let's go, your time's a tickin'."

A man approached the escalator and a small platform ejected from the escalator, he stood on it and was lifted to the second level.

Mike watched him get on the escalator – in amazement.

Down the left hall was 'Room 101 – Information' and next to it 'Room 102 – Records'.

Room 102 was a small, brightly lit room with counters running the full length - wall to wall separating the people and the staff. Two people, sitting at desks, were entering data into computers. To the left was a room - a sign above it, 'TITLE RECORDS SEARCH'. Geoff raised his voice slightly and asked, "can we get some help here?"

A middle aged man looked up, slowly got out of his chair and walked to the counter, "can I help you?"

"Yes, I'd like info on my relatives - they used to live on Mainway Road," Mike said.

"What's their name?"

"Mike Donald senior"

He entered the name in a computer. "No Mike Donald senior, but there's a Mike and Catherine Donald who lived at 1235 Mainway Road - the house changed ownership in 2025."

"What happened to them, where'd they move to?"

"Don't know if they moved, it's the only record displayed – could've moved out of the city."

"Ok," said Mike disenchanted.

"Sorry I couldn't help. You can go to the library and use one of the terminals and search the Internet."

"We'll think about it," said Geoff.

Geoff was determined to get going – back to the SUV. He told Mike they weren't going to the library. Mike did agree – unwillingly. Back at the parking garage, Geoff pressed the unlock button on the remote. Inside the TS, Geoff questioned, "well, what do we do now?" Mike told him to set the return date and press the 'engage' button. Geoff pressed the button and nothing happened. Mike told him to press the button and move the switch also. He moved the switch and nothing happened. Mike noticed that the key was not in the ignition, so Geoff put it in the ignition. He turned the key but the indicator lights didn't come on. He pressed the button again, moved the switch up and the malfunction light came on. Geoff, with both hands, banged on the steering wheel. "Damn, damn, damn, damn."

"Hold it," Mike said. "We won't get any place doing that."

Geoff stopped, looked at Mike. "What the hell do we do now?"

"Were screwed unless there's instructions on how it works, I don't want to be stuck here," said Mike as a look of fear came over his face. Geoff told him to look in the glove box for some sort of instruction book. Mike opened the glove box - there was only the owner's manual.

"Nothing here - what do you suggest we do," said Mike.

"Shut up, let me think," said Geoff angrily.

"Using this time machine was your stupid idea, now we're stuck here," shouted Mike.

Geoff opened the door, got out, stomped his feet and threw up his arms in disgust. Mike got out and walked to the back of the TS. Chris and Jennifer were walking up the parking ramp. Hearing the yelling they cautiously hid behind a van. They peered through the van window at Geoff and Mike arguing.

"They must be trying to leave," said Chris.

"How're we going to get them back – they're violent," said Jennifer.

"Stay down and see what happens."

"You wanted to try this out," said Mike.

"I did not, all I wanted was to know what they were doing."

"Bull Shit to you Geoff," said Mike.

Mike was not backing down, and at the top of his voice. "You always think you're right every time, well this time you really screwed up."

"Screw you, Mike" said Geoff as he grabbed Mike with one hand clenched on his shirt and pushed him against the back of the TS. His hand went back, ready to hit Mike.

"Woh, woh," said Mike as he thought it's no good to provoke Geoff. "We're not going to get out of this mess by fighting."

Geoff released Mike, "what do you suggest, smart ass?"

"Well, let's look in the back, maybe there's something that doesn't look normal."

"What do we know about this SUV," said Geoff as he opened the back. "Can't tell if it's ok or not."

"Wait a minute," said Mike. "Look at this, could've been something in this slot."

"If there was, who could've taken it - the Manlees?" Geoff said in a piercing tone, "and how'd they build another one – that's impossible."

"Ok, Mike lets get a cola and decide what the hell we're going to do."

"We have to think this out, Geoff - how much money do we have?"

"Not much, thirty dollars maybe."

"Let's drive to the Manlee's, maybe we can find something there."

"What could we find there, the place is deserted – let's get a cola and think," said Geoff, "I'm thirsty."

As they left, Chris and Jennifer stayed crouched, moving slowly to the front of the van they were hiding behind. Geoff and Mike were busy talking and walked by the van not noticing them. They heard their first names but didn't really know who they were. They were concerned about bringing them back - how could they get into the TS being so violent – sedate them?

"We need a stun gun." Jennifer said.

CHAPTER 16

August 6, 2104. Geoff and Mike could still be heard in the distance, arguing as they left the parking garage. Cautiously Chris and Jennifer walked to the back of the van, checked down the rows of cars – both ways. That was a close call. Jennifer took another look and couldn't see or hear them any more. They now had to try a sporting goods store for a stun gun. They had to be cautious though, not to run into Mike and Geoff. At the edge of the ramp, they checked around the corner – Mike & Geoff were gone.

"Which way to a sporting goods store?" asked Jennifer.

"Don't know, let's ask this man - he looks like a sportsman."

"What does a sportsman look like?"

"I don't know, check this guy," said Chris.

A man approaching them had on a ball cap with 'BIG FISH CAMPS OF THE WORLD' and 'WE HAVE THE BIG ONES' imprinted on it.

"Ok, but it doesn't prove he's a sportsman."

The man looked at Chris and smiled.

"Excuse me sir, is there a sporting goods store near here?"

"What kind of sporting goods?"

"Hunting, fishing – that type," said Chris.

"The closest one is about eight blocks - it's called 'THE WONDERFUL ALL SPORTS STORE', or as we call it, 'WONDIES'."

He pointed across the street and said, "just go that way - you can't miss 'WONDIES', it's a big store."

"Thanks," said Jennifer with a smile.

He continued on his way, then turned around and waved. Chris smiled and waved back. They followed the directions.

'WONDIES', was a large store, with displays of exercising, fishing and bow hunting in the window.

"People must still like bow hunting - it's sure been around for a long time - centuries," said Chris.

'WONDIES' went 'over board' on their displays. Such realism, displays appeared through the windows.

"That's an interesting exercise machine," said Jennifer.

The words 'TOTAL EXERCISER – ALL YOU NEED,' was flashing in a hologram that extended outside the display window.

The display was a man walking upside down inside a stationary circular cage. The display looked like a hamster cage the man, upside down, had no physical support for the top of the cage. Jennifer being a physicist expressed that it was impossible to do that.

"It's just a hologram, we don't know if it's real or not – probably just advertising," said Chris.

"O…K, let's go ask how it works?"

"We don't have time, maybe on another trip – we have to get the stun guns," said Chris.

"I'm curious; let's go in."

Another display 'caught their eye' - a 'demobilizing' gun stating 'PROTECT YOUR PROPERTY'.

A holographic display showed an intruder in a home, a lady pointed the gun, pulled the trigger; there was a lightning flash. The intruder fell to the floor, stunned, unconscious with sparks bouncing on him.

A banner read, 'THE INTRUDER WILL BE IMMOBILIZED FOR AN HOUR. ENOUGH TIME FOR THE POLICE TO ARRIVE.'

"That's what we need," said Jennifer. "It'll keep them out for the whole trip."

A clerk saw them watching intensely. "That's great for self defense."

"How much?" asked Chris.

"Three hundred and twenty nine dollars - all you need is a valid drivers permit and we can do a police check for you here - you can take it home today."

This was a problem for Chris and Jennifer. How would they give him a driver's permit that was a hundred years old? They would have to get a current permit, but that was probably impossible. Chris was inquisitive of when the guns were originally sold.

"This model has been out for about three months."

"I mean, when did this technology become available?"

The guns came out about thirty years ago, originally for the military and police and about twenty years ago they became available to the public, but didn't work very well. The power supply lasted three shots.

"The current one is a big improvement and it lasts for about fifty shots with a rechargeable energy supply. Do you want one?"

"We'll have to think about it," said Chris.

In a quiet voice Chris said to Jennifer. "Sure would like to get one of those."

"We can't, we'll just have to go back and get something from our time," said Jennifer.

"Let's get the TS, drive back to the house, pick up the suits and devices – we'll go back to two thousand and four, get two stun guns and come back."

"Ok, these units would be much better - ours needs the physical contact and are more difficult to use," said Jennifer.

They left the store, looking out for Mike and Geoff, bypassing all the obvious soda shops. Cautiously walking into the parking garage, they headed to the TS.

Chris opened the door by the remote. Jennifer got in the front seat and put her package on the back seat. She noticed another package there, but didn't open it. Chris put the module into the time unit and installed the relay.

He started the TS and drove it to the exit. The exit screen displayed 'PLEASE DEPOSIT YOUR PARKING PASS INTO THE SLOT." Chris asked if she could see a parking pass. Jennifer looked behind the sun visor and in the glove box – nothing. A display above the slot - 'LOST PARKING PASSES WILL BE CHARGED AT THE FULL RATE. IF YOU LOST YOUR PARKING PASS PRESS THE RED BUTTON.'

He pressed the red button. "YOUR PARKING FOR STALL 15A IS THIRTY SIX DOLLARS. INSERT MONEY CARD OR CASH". Chris got the money card from Jennifer. He put it into the slot, pressed his thumb in the proper place and a receipt was returned. The gate arms went up and they drove out.

Mike and Geoff were walking to the ramp next to the exit.

"That looks like the SUV," said Mike.

"It is, those are the right plates."

"The Manlees must have come here some way," said Geoff.

They ran after the TS not caring what was in the way, knocking over anything including people. The TS got stuck in traffic on Main Street. Chris pressed the lock button and all the doors gave a 'click', almost in harmony as the doors locked. Geoff and Mike caught up to the TS - they banged on the windows and yelled.

"Let us in you asshole," Geoff said, as he was looking Chris in the eyes through the window. Chris smiled and shook his head, 'No'.

Geoff wound up to hit the window with the palm of his right hand but missed and hit the door frame. He pulled back in pain, shook it a few times, and then started using the other hand to bang on the window.

The pain didn't matter as he hit the window with both hands again yelling. "Open the door you assholes."

People started gathering and looking at what was happening. Mike was at the other window banging with his hand, pleading, "Let me in, I don't want to stay here." Geoff was furious and kept banging on the window.

The yelling and banging got the attention of a police cruiser a few cars behind. Two police officers, a man and woman, got out of the car, drew their guns and set them to 'DEMOBILIZE'. Each gun had three settings. 'DEMOBILIZE, STUN, TERMINATE', except for the one officer whose gun had another setting called 'D\CONTROL'. They placed the guns back in the holsters. Reaching back to the car seat they removed a blue ball about four inches in diameter.

The ball had four buttons on it.

DRESS HAT

HELMET

PATROL HAT

COMPACT

Pressing 'Helmet', the ball formed into a helmet which was light blue with a white stripe down the center.

Their uniforms were dark blue, tight fitting, looked like leather, but were very flexible. The jackets matched the color of their uniform. A microphone looking device was clipped to their lapel and a utility pouch loosely clipped to their belt. The pouch contained two demobilizing devices and a pair of handcuffs. The guns looked very square, with various settings. Their nametags read 'Kimberly Doan' and 'Nick Brono'.

Putting the helmets on, they walked to the TS. "You take the passenger window, I'll take the other," said Nick.

They moved quickly through the crowd saying, "get back, this a police matter," and motioned the vehicles to move back giving space around the SUV. The crowd moved back for the police. Some people in the crowd were yelling with a possibility of some getting out of control.

Kim spoke into her lapel microphone.

"This is Doan. We have a Code three (backup required) and Adam twenty two Whiskey Charlie (Possible violent situation with a crowd involved – WC (will confirm)). Two Caucasian men in their twenties." Their location was automatically transmitted to the precinct.

She looked at the TS and could see a man and a woman inside.

"In the vehicle in question there's a Caucasian man and woman in their thirties. We have a gun with D/Control but won't use it unless necessary."

Kim went to the passenger side. Mike was still banging on the window. "Move away from the vehicle."

Mike looked at her, paused for a moment, then continued banging on the window.

"Move away from the vehicle," she repeated.

Mike ignored her and kept on banging on the window, sometimes pausing and saying, "please," to Jennifer.

"Move away from the vehicle or I'll demobilize you."

"They stole our SUV," Mike yelled at her.

"Move away," she said one last time.

Mike wasn't getting any place so he moved away.

"Put your hand on the vehicle and spread your legs."

She got a device out of her utility pouch that looked like a grey colored rope. She placed it around Mike's neck, all of a sudden he calmed down. Everything was very pleasant around him, not a care in the world. (The neck rope was used instead of handcuffs and electronically demobilized the aggressiveness in a person giving them a sense of euphoria).

Taking a scanner from her pocket she moved the scanner over Mike to check for weapons.

She yelled over to Nick, "This one's calm and clean," and took him to the back of the TS.

"Lay on the ground face down," she commanded.

Mike, calm and obedient, did what he was told.

Geoff was still yelling, and banging on the window.

Kim went to the driver's side to help Nick.

"They stole our SUV, we want it back," yelled Geoff.

"Step back," said Nick.

"Screw you, I'm going to get them out," as he banged on the window.

"Back off, put your hands on the vehicle."

"Were not the criminals, they are."

"Put your hands on the vehicle or I'll demobilize you."

"You got the wrong people."

Realizing he's not getting anywhere, and seeing Mike lying on the ground, he finally gave in. He put his hands on the SUV and mumbled, "dumb asses." Kim walked up to Geoff and said in his ear, "did you say something?"

"No, just clearing my throat."

She put a calming rope on Geoff, and he became placid. After scanning him for weapons, she took him behind the TS and told him to lie on the ground, face down. Geoff did it willingly.

During this time Chris set the return date to August 28, 2004, 8 pm. He pressed the return button for time travel just in case they had to get out of this situation fast. All that was left to do was move the switch.

Nick was at the driver's window. "Come out of the vehicle." He placed his left hand on the door handle trying to open it. "Open the door and come out of the vehicle," he ordered.

Chris looked at Nick, saw his nametag and said, "This isn't a good situation," and moved the switch.

Nick saw Chris move the switch, "Put your hands on the dash, both of you - don't touch anything or I'll shoot."

The back of the TS glowed bright blue, then faded into time travel.

CHAPTER 17

August 6, 2104. It was late afternoon when the sequence initiated for time travel with Nick still holding onto the door handle being 'dragged' back in time. Just into the time travel Nick's legs suddenly shot up putting him in a horizontal position. He managed to put the gun in the holster and grabbed the side mirror. Terrified – no - he was traumatized - 'what's going on' while getting bombarded with the weather changes. The 'whine' from the TS was abnormally high. Chris and Jennifer had to talk louder, but not shouting because of the noise.

"Why's he in that position," said Jennifer.

"Don't know, the movement of time must be so fast it's trying to pull him off – I thought anybody near the TS would be dragged along."

The area was reversing in time, buildings were changing, night and day were moving rapidly, people and cars moving through them at high speeds. Rain, hail, thunderstorms, hot spells and snow were experienced for very short periods.

"Why haven't the cars affected us?" asked Jennifer.

"It's a short time, they can't materialize enough, it could be a problem 'though if we were going slower."

"What about the weather?"

"The weather is for longer periods, did you notice how long we stay wet, with rain or snow - rain appears and disappears slower because we're not moving fast."

This time it was happening slower than his 1971 trip. Chris hoped that they don't have any problems – it could be serious if they materialized in the street at a different time period.

Nick, with a horrified look, mouthed to Chris as to what's going on. Chris looked at him, shrugged his shoulders - he couldn't do anything. The time indicator was moving backward .... 2101 - 2095 – 2089 along with the months, days and hours. The TS began to shake, from the back a crackling sound, like electric arcs.

Jennifer was frightened; she looked at Chris, "What's going on?"

Chris looked at her. "The insulator is still a problem on the initial burst voltage - that's why we're traveling slowly. It should stop once the voltage stabilizes."

He looked at the malfunction light it wasn't 'ON'. 'That's a break,' he thought.

"Watch the time indicators - if he lets go we can come back and get him."

Nick, with a ghastly look, was still getting bombarded with the weather changes. His communicator and utility pouch had just fallen off. Jennifer looked at the indicator. It was January 15, 2073 at about 1 am. Just as she was about to say the time, Nick lost his grip on the door handle and mirror and faded into another time.

"There he goes, what's the date?" asked Chris.

"May 16, 2072 about 3 pm"

A few seconds later the initial burst was over, the 'whine' softened and the TS stabilized but was still slow.

Jennifer looked at Chris, "I don't like this - if the TS goes this slow, I don't want to go very far from our home time."

"Once I find the proper insulator, the problem will be solved - I'll check with Rich when we get back, he should know what's available for insulators."

"Hope everything's ok," said Jennifer.

"It is, if the voltage is low, the time trip will only take longer."

The energy gauge was normal. The voltage, with no gauge, could be low.

When did Nick fall? In seventy-two she said, if he's more than thirty it'll be around the time he was born. Nick was a few years old in 2072 and would know someone there – his parents, they would be younger than him.

"We'll have to come back and get Nick," said Jennifer.

"Right, we shouldn't leave him there - poor guy, hope he manages to survive."

They talked about the look on his face and laughed, not at Nick, but the situation he was in.

"He didn't know what was happening," said Chris with a smile on his face.

"We shouldn't laugh, but it was funny," said Jennifer.

"Did you see him going through the rain and hail - that really confused him."

As they approached their home time the TS became transparent and rapidly 'floated' towards their home. The surroundings changed slower; there was that floating sensation again.

"What's happening now?"

"We're heading for home – it'll only last a short time.

People in the streets and in cars saw the TS appear as a transparent, ghostly image, rapidly floating out of the city. Drivers became disorientated causing minor crashes.

In a short time they materialized in the TS building.

CHAPTER 18

August 28, 2004. It was early evening. They sat in the TS for a few minutes, happy they were back but not saying much. They looked at each other with a feeling nothing was really accomplished except getting the TS back.

Now there was Nick in 2072, how to get Geoff and Mike back from 2104 and keep them quiet about the TS. Jennifer, thinking so much of all these situations, forgot to tell Chris the date and time Nick's communicator and utility pouch fell off in 2073, although it was of minor importance.

"We have a mess to resolve, if we hadn't built this damned machine we wouldn't have these problems." She was on the verge of crying, but held back.

"It wasn't our fault - how could've we known the TS would be stolen - we still have to correct these situations

- solving the insulator problem has to be our first priority, then we can go back and correct the future."

Jennifer retracted what she had said, "I didn't really mean 'not building the TS' - I'd just like to time travel and do some normal things such as sight seeing, shopping in the future – maybe even seeing the past, some history." She smiled at Chris. He smiled, put his arm around her. "After these situations are solved we will be able to do just that."

"Well, we'd better get the packages out of here and something to eat."

Chris removed the keys from the ignition and reached for the packages behind the back seat. It didn't strike him immediately there was a second package. He got out of the TS, closed the door and put the packages on the table. One package had Jennifer's jeans and the two magnetic umbrellas. The package was soft, but the other package wasn't.

Jennifer got out of the TS and closed the door. "Give me the package and I'll take it in the house."

"There's two packages," he said.

"Where'd the other package come from, I don't remember us buying anything else," she said.

Jennifer walked to the table and opened the package with the books. They looked at the book covers, one on autos and the other on company performance. Chris picked up the company performance book and looked at it.

"They were going to profit from this book."

"We have to get rid of it – this is worse than insider trading."

He set the book on the table and picked up the other book, "This is an interesting one."

He opened it and up popped a display. Projected above the book was a menu with multiple 2104 cars, trucks, and SUVs listed and the instructions on how to use the book. He read the instructions.

'This 'SPORTS UTILITY VEHICLE – MODEL FSU501' looks interesting." He pressed 'SPORTS UTILITY VEHICLE – MODEL FSU501'.

A hologram popped up, gave a short summary of the vehicle, and then gave a demo of the SUV in a test drive simulation featuring the advanced guidance system.

A banner ran along the bottom.

'THE MODEL FSU501 IS READY FOR THE NEXT PHASE OF ENERFUEL AND HAS THE ADVANCED GUIDANCE SYSTEM.'

The advanced guidance system controlled its travel over the blue lines on the road, stopping at 'STOP' signs and speeding and slowing depending on road conditions. It turned onto a road with only the center and outside lane markers.

'THE ONBOARD SENSORS CAN NOW MONITOR 360 DEGREES, KEEPING THE FSU501 ACCIDENT PROOF.'

The display continued, showing it going towards a 'washed out' bridge. It stopped well before, and on the dash displayed, 'BRIDGE INOPERATIVE AHEAD'. (Geoff had looked at a similar demo.)

"That's quite the technology," said Chris. "There's a mention of enerfuel, wonder what it is?"

"Probably some future fuel, did you notice how quiet the cars were - maybe it's the fuel they use?"

Under 'INDEX' there was 'TERMS AND DESCRIPTIONS'.

He scrolled down to enerfuel.

'ENERFUEL – ENERFUEL IS MADE BY BREAKING THE H_2O (WATER) BOND THROUGH A CATALYTIC REACTION TO PRODUCE A CONTROLLED RATE OF ELECTRICAL ENERGY.

BY PRODUCTS ARE HYDROGEN AND OXYGEN WITH NO HEAT PRODUCED. THE OLDER ENERFUEL REQUIRED TREATED WATER WITH FREE HYDROGEN AND A RADIATOR FOR COOLING. THE NEW ENERFUEL USES NORMAL WATER AND PRODUCES RELATIVELY NO HEAT.'

"Sounds like some form of fusion," said Jennifer, "I'm going in, want a sandwich?"

"Sure, you know this enerfuel would probably work better than the laser capacitors. Too bad it's not available."

"Are you coming?"

"Make the sandwiches and I'll be in shortly."

"Ok, they'll be ready in fifteen minutes, come in by that time."

He put the book on the table. "Just going to take a look at the insulator - won't be too long."

Jennifer was going towards the man door, stopped and pointed to the roll up door, "You're going to have to fix the door soon."

"I'll get some new panels tomorrow."

He plugged in a portable light, took it to the TS, opened the back and placed it beside the insulator cover. After removing the cover he looked at the insulator and the control modules. The control unit was ok. The insulator had the same problems as before – electrical arcing and carbon deposits. Removing the insulator he set it on the table.

His brother should know what insulators are available. He works at a utility company that uses many of them. 'I'll phone Rich tomorrow' he thought, probably should have talked to him first. Taking the light from the back of the TS he unplugged it, used the remote control to lock the TS and went into the house. The kitchen clock showed 11:22 pm. On the table was the sandwich, covered in plastic wrap. Only the kitchen lights were on, he assumed Jennifer went to bed.

"I guess she knows me now – getting involved with the TS and not paying attention to time." The fifteen minutes had stretched to over three hours. He got a glass of water, sat down at the table and ate the sandwich. After finishing he sat there for a few minutes then went to bed.

CHAPTER 19

August 29, 2004. It was early morning; Jennifer awoke, rolled over to her side, and looked at the clock. It was after 7:30 am, she yawned and rolled onto her back. Chris was stirring a little and started to awaken. He blinked his eyes a few times then opened them. Sunlight was coming through a split in the curtains, dimly lighting the room.

"Was that a dream?" asked Jennifer.

"Wish it was."

"Have to fix those situations, we're going to have to go back and pick up those portable time devices first," she said, "after the insulator is fixed."

Chris would have to phone his brother and find out if he can help him find an insulator. He should have called him when he had the problem originally.

"Well, let's have some breakfast," as Jennifer got out of bed and opened the curtains.

Chris put his hand up to shade his eyes, but stayed in bed thinking of all that had happened and how to correct it all. After doing the morning rituals they went downstairs to the kitchen. Jennifer filled the coffee pot and turned it on. During their first cup, they sat at the table talking about the time travel troubles.

"Any solutions of how to fix the problems – especially on bringing back Mike and Geoff and keeping them quiet?" asked Jennifer.

"No, that one is going to be tough to solve, we should just leave them there. Hope Nick is ok."

"I don't know where he would land, it could be anywhere or at the place we started from in the street."

"If he ended up in the street, there would be traffic and he could get hurt - I hate to think what could happen."

"He'll be ok," said Chris. "Anyway, we'll find out when we go back to get him."

"We are going back – that's definite?"

"Yes" said Chris.

"I agree, what about Geoff and Mike - I think that was their names."

"We'll go back and get them - on second thought, if we left them there the problem would be solved," he continued.

"When we go back and get Nick, he might have some ideas on how we can solve the Geoff and Mike problem," said Jennifer.

"If he's willing after all that's happened, anyway, where do we find him, is he ok, is he still alive?" queried Chris.

Jennifer was at the stove cooking breakfast and turned to Chris. "This wouldn't have happened if Geoff and Mike weren't so nosey".

Breakfast was ready; she put it on the table and sat down, and took a sip of coffee.

"Well, if I can get help from Rich on the insulator, we can probably leave in a few days; we'll get Nick first, then the other two."

After breakfast, Chris went back to the TS building. One computer with a broken cable needed to be fixed. Removing the connector from the computer he opened it up. Two wires were broken. He soldered the connections and attached it back to the computer. Jennifer came into the building, walked up to Chris, "should get the door fixed, Chris."

"I was going to do that after I fixed this cable - I'll go where we originally got the door, they should have replacement panels. You know, with the problems we had with the break-ins, I'll get a security system as well."

Chris got up and went to the file cabinet, found the instructions for the door and checked the model number. The model number was there, but he decided to take the complete manual with him, 'just to make sure he got the proper parts'. He drove to the lumber store. At the front counter there was a clerk and her nametag said 'Stephanie'. He asked if they had replacement panels for garage doors.

"What's the model number and size?"

Chris gave her the manual.

"Oh, that's a model number M250016GS – 16 foot wide door."

At the computer she entered the number.

"Yes, we do have the panels in stock, sixteen foot galvanized steel, unpainted - how many do you need?"

"Five"

"What happened to them?" she inquired.

"Oh, they got damaged a while ago, thought it's time to replace them."

"Do you want them installed?"

"No, I'll do it myself, thanks."

"Did the panel bracing get damaged?"

"Yes, guess I'll need a set for each panel – include the bolts and attachment hardware also."

She suggested he buy a complete new door as all the parts were included and would be cheaper. Chris thought it was a good idea; he would have the panels, nuts and bolts and wouldn't have to make a trip back if there was anything short. She asked him if he had installed a door before. He replied 'No'. Their installers could do it for him. Chris said he would try it himself first.

"Let me check the delivery schedule." She went to the computer; "the earliest is tomorrow morning about 11 am."

"That'll do."

He paid for the door and she thanked him. The next stop was the Mall for an alarm system. The mall directory listed a security store - 'HIGH TECH SECURITY SUPPLIES – FIRST LEVEL – STORE 108'. The direction was to the left, eight stores down. Entering the store he saw a customer at the counter and one sales clerk. All types of systems were displayed. There was information on the system.

THIS SYSTEM IS THE MOST HIGH TECH AND FOOL PROOF SECURITY SYSTEM FOR DETERING OF INTRUDERS. THE LASERS USED ARE NOT VISIBLE TO THE HUMAN EYE. THE SYSTEM IS EASY TO INSTALL AND OPERATES ON A WIRELESS RADIO BAND AT 2.4 GHZ FOR THE BEST RECEPTION. THE SIGNAL CAN PENITRATE WALLS AND IS RECEIVALBE UP TO 500 FT. THE SYSTEM OPERATES ON A RECHARGEABLE BATTERY AND IS IMMUNE TO POWER FAILURES. FULLY TAMPER PROOF. DESIGNED BY SECURITY SCIENTISTS. The customer left and the clerk walked over to Chris.

"Can I help you?"

"How good are these security systems?" as he pointed to the laser systems.

"Top of the line - works on the same principal that's used in high security places such as in the government buildings. All you have to do is set them up at the doors and all windows in your home."

"I'll need it for a garage."

It even worked better for a garage - all he needed is one for each door and any group of windows. In a home there's was more chance of false alarms such as people getting up in the middle of the night, pets and that sort of thing. Chris asked about the monitoring panel. It came in two, six, twelve and thirty-six monitoring points and could be connected for local alarm or call out to a security service. They could even recommend one for him. A four-hour battery was used in case of power failure.

"Do all the points have to be hooked up?"

"No, just connect the ones you want and make them active."

Chris asked how it was set up. To set it up, all that was needed was a minimal knowledge of computers, 'enough to pick from a menu'. Additional modules were available for up to six remote cameras and two remote TV monitors. The cameras were the 'low light', infrared type. Chris was satisfied that these would work, and bought a thirty six point monitor, twenty four sensors, four IR cameras and the required interface modules.

"Don't think we have all in stock, but let me check."

He went to the computer and entered the part numbers.

They had the sensors, one remote TV, two IR cameras and two low light cameras in stock. The other parts, including the panel, were stocked in the California warehouse – he could get them overnight and have them delivered tomorrow.

"I'll take the ones you have in stock, call me when the other parts come in and I'll pick them up."

"Ok, I'll total this up."

"Will need your name, address and phone number."

Chris gave him the information, paid with his credit card, pickup up a box of parts and left.

As he was leaving the clerk said, "will call you when the rest comes in, and thanks."

It was 6:00 in the evening; Chris and Jennifer were in the kitchen.

Chris was happy with all he accomplished today – at least he got the items ordered. His first job was to get the door fixed. After dinner Chris called Rich about the insulator. He dialed the number, it rang twice and Donna answered the phone.

"Hello," she said.

"Hello, how are you?" Chris asked.

"Fine, anything exciting happen lately?"

"Too much"

"Made two trips with the TS and had some interesting experiences."

"What type of experiences?"

"Saw mom and dad then went to 2104."

"Wow, must have been exciting, did Jennifer go?"

"She went on the future one, but not to the past – both were unplanned, we had problems with some guys. They broke into the garage."

"What do you mean unplanned? Who broke into the garage?"

"It's a long story – the next time we get together we'll explain everything that happened - Is Rich there?"

"Yes, I'll get him."

Chris could hear, "Rich, your brother is on the phone."

"Be right there." He heard footsteps, "Hi Chris, how's it going - is the TS ready yet?"

"Yes and we had some interesting experiences - saw mom and dad and also went to 2104. Both trips were unplanned because of snoopy guys. We have to go back to 2072 and 2104 for some unfinished business."

"Need any help?"

"I do, but not to travel, what I need is a good insulator for the TS. I had the INSULATION TECHNIQUES 110, but got tracking on it, any suggestions?"

"There are a few rated higher – a model 125 and 135 – I'll check tomorrow if you like."

"Can you order the best rated one for me and have it sent over night?"

"I'll see what I can do, shouldn't be a problem."

"Did Jennifer go?"

"She did on the trip to the future - on the first I ended up in 1972 and saw mom and dad."

"They didn't believe who I was at first - I think mom knew or had a feeling it was me, anyway they sent you, Donna and John their love after I told them about you, I also have a letter from dad, which I'll send you."

"Did you warn them about the accident?"

"No, they didn't want to change the inevitable. I had a problem and left in a hurry, didn't get to pursue it with them."

"Too bad, I'd like to see them, maybe we can plan a trip."

"After I get this insulator problem and the other screw-ups solved we'll plan a trip, maybe all five of us can go. You realize when we go back to 1971, mom and dad will be younger than us."

"Yes, but I guess we can work around that."

"Got to go, I'll call later when everything is settled," Chris said.

"Chris, I'll email you when I find out about the insulators and when you can expect them to be delivered."

Jennifer was standing beside Chris and whispered in his ear, "Let me talk to Donna."

"Rich, can you put Donna on the phone for Jennifer?"

He called to her, "Jennifer wants to talk to you."

Chris handed Jennifer the phone. "Hello"

Rich was still there. "Quite the adventures you guys are having."

"Tell me about it - wish we could have more 'normal' trips."

Donna walked up to Rich, he said 'Donna's here' and handed her the phone.

"Hello, Jennifer, exciting things have happened from what Chris was telling us."

"Yes, but I wanted to tell you about the interesting jeans I bought in 2104. They're adjustable for style and color automatically. You'll have to see them the next time we visit."

"That sounds great, did you do any other shopping there?"

"A little, I'd like to go back under better circumstances."

"Let's plan a trip soon."

"We will, after we get the problems solved."

"Got to go, we're just having dinner. Rich said he'll email Chris tomorrow."

"Ok, Love to all of you and a special one to John."

"And to you and Chris"

They hung up the phones. Chris had a lot of work to do, fixing the door and a new insulator for the TS. If Rich found a reliable one the continuous problem of the insulator could be solved.

CHAPTER 20

May 16, 2072. It was early afternoon when Nick appeared in the isle of a school bus, lying on the floor. Realizing this he hurriedly got up. This was the same spot where he lost his grip on the door handle when he was being transported from the future. The school bus, with eight-year-old school kids as passengers, was stopped for a traffic light. The kids started to scream. Nick immediately motioned with his arms out and hands up to calm down. Almost as fast as they started screaming, they stopped. The driver, a lady in her early forties looked in the rear view mirror and got up to see what was going on. The kids started asking Nick questions.

One of the boys saw his gun in the holster said, “can I see your gun, is it real?”

“No, just a practice gun, it’s only set to demobilize.”

"What's demobilize?"

Nick thinking he should down play this said, "It's like a toy gun."

"Can I see it?"

He took his helmet off and pressed 'Dress Hat', all of a sudden the helmet formed a hat. He put it on.

"Cool, how'd you do that, are you a magician?" asked another boy.

Before he could answer, he got another question.

A girl questioned, "were you hiding in the back?"

Another boy asked, "are you a ghost?"

Nick, thinking fast said, "no, I'm on a special assignment."

"What does that mean?" asked the girl.

Nick's back was to the front of the bus. Before he could answer the question there was a 'tap, tap, tap' on his shoulder.

"How'd you get in here?"

Nick turned around, gave a grin and said, "I'm a police officer."

She looked down at his side and saw a holstered gun. "You can't have a gun on a school bus, who are you anyway and how did you get on the bus?"

"I'm a police officer," he repeated and pointed to his badge.

"Sure haven't seen any police officer's dressed like you before, what's your badge number?"

"AC 531982," he said. "This is a new uniform, I'm one of the first to try it out."

The boy that asked if he was a magician said, "he can do tricks, he made his hat change."

She looked at the boy. "What do you mean change?"

"It can be changed into the type needed," Nick explained.

She looked back at him and raised an eyebrow.

"I don't know what's going on here, I'll have to call dispatch."

"Your name is Nick Brono," as she read it from his nametag.

"Yes"

The light had changed to green and the cars in front of the bus had moved. The cars behind the bus started honking. "Get that thing moving," could be heard from the people yelling from the cars. Nick asked her to open the door so he could get out.

"How did you get in here?"

The cars behind honked again and drivers shouted, "Move the bus, get that bus moving."

Nick continued to explain to the driver. "This is a new routine drill to respond for assisting people."

"I wasn't told of anything like this."

"Its top secret," as he moved past her, up to the front, he opened the door and jumped out of the bus. The driver, a bit dumfounded, saw him run into a back alley and out of view.

She lost sight of him and thought that this was a bizarre situation. Luckily the kids are alright. "I'll radio in and report this."

She went to the front and picked up the microphone.

The door was still open and two people came to the door.

"Is everything ok, do you want us to call the police?"

"No, everything's ok, nothing to worry about."

She closed the door and continued to drive the bus. She pressed the talk switch on the microphone and asked if dispatch was there. Dispatch acknowledged.

"Had a strange situation here," as she thought for a minute and wondered if she told them what happened – would they believe her?

"Um ...... um, I'll explain when I get in - everything Ok."

Dispatch questioned if she was Ok. She acknowledged that she was and she would file a report when she got back. The indicators had shown that she had spent longer than normal time at Main and Statewide Streets.

"Right," she replied and added, "will tell you when I get back."

"Ok, I'll record there was an incident, are you sure everything is ok!"

"Yes"

The kids on the bus were still talking to each other about what happened. One of the kids said, "he's probably from the future – just like the movies."

The kid was right, but Nick didn't realize he was in 2072. He did wonder where he was, everything looked kind off familiar, but strange almost if he went back in time. How did he get on the school bus? Why did he materialize there? Did the people in the SUV have something to do with this? The bus driver didn't recognize him as a police officer. He took his jacket off and placed his badge, nametag and gun with the holster in it and rolled it up. He returned the hat to the ball form and placed it in the jacket as well. He returned to the street. The cars were a lot different from what he was used to. The newspaper boxes didn't have a screen on them showing the headlines, but just an ordinary box with the big window showing the front of the paper and a date of Monday, May 16, 2072. He opened his eyes startled and shook his head, then bent down to look at the date again.

"What's going on here?" He looked at a car parked on the street and walked closer to get a look at the license plate - 'EXPIRE 02/73'.

He realized he had been transported to the past and the vehicle he was holding onto got him here. How was he going to get back to his future!

"I was born in 2069, that'll make me about three years old. The only choice I have is to go home and see if my parents can help."

Nick's parents lived in the suburbs, still living in the same house as in 2104. He thought of taking a cab to the house, but all he had was a money card, no cash. Would cash be any good even if he had some, probably not – he was technically broke. The only way to get to his parent's home was to walk then hitch a ride when he got to the main road. When he got to the main road leading out of the city he tried flagging a car. Eventually one stopped and the driver rolled down the passenger side window. "Are you a military man?"

"I've been in the army."

The driver was in his early twenties, dark brown hair and had a neatly trimmed mustache.

"How far you goin'?"

"To the Washington Drive exit."

"Well hop in, it's just a few miles down the road and it's the one I'm turning on, any particular place?"

The car door opened and Nick got in. There was the old automatic guidance system, not what Nick was used to, but the driver preferred the manual mode.

"Where ya going?"

"1595 Washington Road," said Nick.

"Damn, that's where I'm staying with my brother's family, are you a friend of the Brono's?"

"Well sort of, it's a long story, what's your name?"

"Adam Brono."

Nick thought, "there was an Adam Brono, who went to the conflict in '75 and never returned - he's my uncle."

Nick looked at him. "What kind of work do you do?"

"Military, leaving next week for specialty training with the Rangers."

Nick asked him how long he had been in the military. Two years, next month he said.

"How do you like it?"

"It's my career, it's great."

Adam asked Nick what he did. Nick said a police officer from California – LA. It was the only thing he could think of not wanting to say he was from the local city. Adam commented that the uniform 'sort of' looked like it was police or military, but he hadn't seen that type before. It's a new type being tested Nick responded.

"How come you're still wearing it?"

"Uh ...., uh ...., it's................., it's just comfortable and I usually get a ride easier if I have it on."

"What you got in the bag, or is it your jacket?"

"Just some personal stuff and my jacket"

"Where's your suitcase?"

"Got lost"

"Up here for a visit or on business?"

"A visit"

"How are you related to Jim?"

"I'm a cousin of Jim (Jim was his father), about a fourth cousin," he said making up whatever came into his head.

"Have you been here before?"

"No, I just wanted to see some of Oregon, so I came here for a vacation."

"Well we're here," as he drove into the driveway.

Adam got out of the car, but Nick still sat there wondering what he was going to say or do. Are you coming in Adam asked?

"Oh.............., uh........, yes.................," as he grabbed his bundled jacket and got out of the car.

They walked up to the door, went in. He set his jacket beside the door, looked around, it was very familiar, just as if he had been there yesterday. Nick's mom Tania was busy in the kitchen, when she heard them she came out. Beside her was a small boy.

"Hello, I'm Tania and this is Nick."

"I'm Nick also, from California - just visiting to see my long lost cousin Jim."

He walked up to Tania and shook her hand. It was odd, looking at his mother who was younger than he was.

He reached down to shake little Nick's hand. When they got within six inches of each other a lightning bolt sparked between their hands.

He pulled back. "Wow, must be a lot of static electricity in here."

The incident caused a blister to form on the palm of both of their hands. Little Nick started to cry violently, almost screaming. Tania picked him up and gently rocked him side to side saying, "it'll be ok, it'll be ok."

Nick shook his hand from the pain.

"Damn, that's the worst static I've seen," Nick said.

The thought went through his mind, maybe, he couldn't be with himself in the same time and place. He had to be careful. He looked at his hand and a scar was in the same spot where little Nick got zapped along with a new blister.

"That's a bad blister." As she looked at little Nick's hand.

"I'll take him upstairs and get something for it – he probably needs a nap anyway."

Little Nick was still sobbing as she took him upstairs saying again. "That's sure a nasty blister on your hand, mommy will get something for it."

"That's a bad one you have on your hand – do you want me to get you something for it?" asked Adam.

Nick was still in a pain. He asked if he could get some antiseptic and a bandage. Adam took him to the bathroom near the kitchen and put some antiseptic and a bandage on it. Adam commented that it was like – using my military medic training, and laughed. Nick thanked him for the good job he did.

"Want something to eat or drink, I'm going to make a sandwich."

"Do you have a beer, sure could use one?"

"What kind do you want?"

"Whatever you have will be fine."

He brought the beer, handed it to Nick and said he had to go out for fifteen minutes. He had a sandwich in his hand and was eating it as he walked to the door. About ten minutes later Tania came down from upstairs.

"That was a real nasty blister. I haven't seen anything like that before."

"What did you say your name was?"

"Nick."

A coincidence, both their names were the same she thought. She asked what Nick's last name was and how was he was related to Jim. Nick almost said he was his father, but quickly changed it to his cousin, fourth removed.

"How long are you here for?"

"Just a few days"

"Where are you staying?"

"Haven't got a place yet"

Tania didn't know if she should ask him to stay but thought, since he's supposed to be a relative, she told him 'if he wanted, there was a bedroom just off the kitchen' he could use. Nick was very appreciative and thanked her. He didn't know where he'd stay because he didn't know anyone in the city and his money card from the future wasn't any good. Tania said that Jim should be home in an hour – had Nick met him before.

"No, but I can hardly wait."

Tania felt she knew him for some reason; he must be more than a cousin of Jim's. She asked about his parents and Nick made up a fictitious name of Anthony and Allison, that's all he could think of on the spur of the moment. She said that Jim never mentioned them before.

"They're fourth removed, I guess they didn't talk too much, or even write."

"Where are your parents now?"

"Oh, they died."

"How did they die?"

"Uh……, Uh…… a car accident"

"How long ago?"

"Oh, about fifteen years ago."

"I guess that's why we never heard from them, they must have been older than Jim."

"Ya, that's probably the reason."

Nick had to think of something to stop the questioning. Tania kept asking questions and he had to keep making up 'lies', but what could he do? He asked to use the bathroom, and would stay in there for quite a while, at least fifteen minutes or 'till Jim got home. He went into the bathroom and just sat there. Should he tell Jim what happened? Jim, as his dad was a level headed person and could analyze things very well, but how would he react to 'time travel'? Guess he'll find out, he had to tell him to get some help. About 5:10 pm Jim came home. He walked in the door and Tania said, "you have a relative visiting, his name is Nick and he said his parents were Allison and Anthony, did you know them?"

"Haven't heard of an Allison, did have an Uncle Anthony, I think he lived in the mid west some place."

"He said his parents had lived in California but died about fifteen years ago."

"Could've had some relatives there, but haven't heard of any in California."

Nick heard a man talking so he left the bathroom, walked out to the kitchen where Jim was sitting in a chair next to Tania.

"Hi," Nick said.

"Hello," said Jim.

"Can we go outside and talk," said Nick as he walked up to Jim to shake his hand.

"Ok, what happened to your hand?"

"Static electricity"

They went outside to the front step. Jim was wondering why he wanted to talk outside. Nick explained to Jim that he was his son from the future and he didn't know how he got there.

"I'm a police officer and was stopping a disturbance in the city and the date was August 6, 2104."

"Hold on now, are you telling me you traveled here from the future - that's not possible." Nick didn't think he could travel from the future but here he was. Jim wasn't sure – how could he be his son from the future?

"Well, when I was about to shake little Nick's hand, a spark jumped across our hands and gave him a blister - this scar on my hand is identical, we're both the same people, only I'm a lot older."

"How do I know that, did anyone see it?" Nick said that Tania and Adam saw it.

"Ok, I'll ask them."

They went inside and Tania was sitting in a living room chair. Jim said he had a peculiar situation to tell her – this Nick was their son from the future - when he touched little Nick, a spark from his hand gave Nick a blister and did that happen?

"It did, how can he be our son, our son is upstairs having a nap?"

"I'm here from the future, since Nick and I are the same person, there seems to be electricity or something between us."

"This is hard to believe, nobody travels from the future," said Tania.

Just then Adam walked in the front door.

"Did you hear that," said Jim.

"Hear what?"

"Nick is little Nick but from the future."

Adam started to laugh and said, "You're putting me on, that's impossible."

"No" said Nick. "For some reason I was transported from 2104 to here."

"Your clothes look a little odd; I guess traveling in a police uniform is also unusual."

"Just a minute, I'll show you my gun, badge and name tag from 2104. Better still I'll show you my drivers permit." Adam perked up when Nick mentioned a Gun. He wanted to see it being a military man. Adam and Nick walked to where he left his jacket. Adam was inquisitive as to the type of gun.

"It's the latest from 2104, a type of static ray gun, with the latest features, including crowd control. You can set it from demobilize to kill - right now it's set for demobilize. It only works in my hand."

"Can I see it?" asked Adam.

They walked to where Jim and Tania were sitting, Adam holding the gun and Nick holding his rolled up jacket and all the items inside. Tania expressed that she didn't like guns and to take it outside. Jim suggested to go to the back yard. Nick grabbed his jacket, Adam carried the gun and being a military man was curious to see how it worked. Nick took the gun and explained the features of it.

"That's quite a weapon, bet the military would like to get some of these."

"The military has much more advanced ones in 2104."

"Are you going back to the future, and how are you going to do it?"

"Don't know or even how, I might be stuck here."

The front door bell rang and it was three police officers. Tania answered it and asked what they required. They said they were looking for a Nick Brono. She said he was upstairs having a nap. They wanted to talk to him and if she would wake him up.

"He's only three years old what could he have done?"

"The person we are looking for is in his early thirties, the name given to us was Nick Brono."

Jim heard someone talking, and went into the house. At the front door he introduced himself as Jim Brono and asked if he could help them. They said they were looking for a Nick Brono that was about five feet ten inches tall, in his early thirties.

"Why?" Jim asked.

"He was on a school bus with a gun. We'd like to question him."

"Yes, there's a Nick Brono in the back that fits that description, shall I get him?"

The police officers drew their guns out of their holsters.

"No, we'll go and get him."

Nick was holding his gun in his hand. The police saw the gun and said. "Drop the weapon and put your hands up."

Nick did as they said. They came over and searched him, handcuffed him and said he would have to come with them for questioning. A police officer grabbed Nick's jacket with all the other items. They drove to the police station and took him to the interrogation room.

Inside the room was a chair that had a computer type of screen on either side of the chair. Two police officers were in the room, 'John Potts and James Ballard'. The handcuffs were removed and Nick was told to sit in the chair. He was asked if he was familiar with the function of this chair?

"Looks familiar ----- somewhat," said Nick.

"I'll explain it to you anyway," said John. "The identifier chip you have in your neck will give us a profile of you. Just sit back in the chair."

John turned the machine on and the screens displayed a series of ones and zeros. (Nick's identifier chip was a newer version that the machine couldn't read.)

"The machine or your identifier chip must be faulty," said John, "we'll do this manually. Do you know why you're here?"

"No, not exactly," said Nick.

"We got a call this afternoon and obtained a statement from a bus driver that you were on a school bus with a gun. Is that true?"

Nick hesitated and said he had nothing to hide. "Yes, but I can explain."

"Did you know in this state it's a felony?"

"Yes," said Nick.

"Where are you from?" asked John.

"Right here from the city."

"Where do you live?"

"I don't really know. It probably is 1595 Washington Road.

"What do you mean probably?"

"It's a long story."

"Well, we have time," said James.

Nick told them he was from the future and what had happened including materializing in the bus.

"You say you are from the future, right," said James.

"How did you get here?"

"It's as I was holding the handle of an SUV at a traffic dispute when everything happened."

"Do you have any proof?"

"Get my wallet and I'll show you."

James got his wallet and Nick got out his drivers permit. The permit stated 'EXPIRY 04/2106'. The picture on the permit was odd, it rotated to show a full profile of Nick's head at all angles when a tab on it labeled 'PROFILE' was pressed. When they pressed 'VITAL DATA' all the data on Nick started to scroll slowly, from his health condition to his duties as a police officer.

"Looks pretty impressive, but this isn't a valid driver's permit, it's some sort of high tech toy," said James.

"That's enough, were booking you for possession of a weapon on a school bus."

They read him his rights. "Legal council will be assigned to you tomorrow," said James.

"You will be detained and formally charged tomorrow. A bail hearing will be after you are formally charged. Do you have anything to say?"

"No," he said, "I'm telling the truth."

They took Nick to a cell. Another man was there as well lying on a bed. He gave Nick a grin when the officer put him in the cell. The man sat up, smiled and asked what he did to get arrested. Nick told him he had caused a disturbance.

"They usually don't throw anyone in here for a disturbance unless there was fighting or resisting arrest."

"No fighting or resisting, but they suspect I had a weapon."

"What kind of weapon."

"A gun."

"Where did you have the gun, do you have a permit to carry one?"

"No, it was on a school bus."

"Pretty stupid thing to do, they'll throw the book at you."

"I know but it was an unavoidable situation."

"Anyway, if nobody got hurt you'll only get ten years," as he laughed and lay down on the bed.

Jim and Adam asked if they could see him. Yes, they were told, but tomorrow morning. They walked to the car and while driving home found it hard to believe all that had happened that evening.

"Wonder what's going to happen to him," said Adam.

"Don't know, the question is how is he going to get back to the future, if that's where he's from? If he's found guilty he'd have to spend some time in jail – he could get stuck here."

CHAPTER 21

August 30, 2004. It was early morning just after eight. The sun was shining through an open spot in the window curtains, onto the mirror on the far wall and reflected back into Jennifer's eyes. She rubbed her eyes and blinked a few times. Sure didn't sleep well, too much on my mind. She looked at the clock and it was 8:12 am.

"Are you awake?" she asked as she turned to Chris, and propped herself up on one elbow.

"What time is it?" Chris replied.

"Twelve after eight."

"Did you sleep well?" she asked.

"No, didn't get much sleep, I kept thinking about Nick and how we're going to get Mike and Geoff back," he said, "I kept wondering how Nick is."

Chris sat up, put his feet on the floor, but didn't get up. He stretched his arms above his head and yawned.

"We'd better plan something for tomorrow's trip," Jennifer said. She got up, put on her housecoat and went down stairs.

Chris lay back on the bed, his feet still on the floor, and fell asleep again. She put the coffee pot on and called to Chris. "What do you want for breakfast?"

No response. Calling again in a louder tone, "what do you want for breakfast?"

No response. She went upstairs; Chris was sleeping again in an uncomfortable position. She moved his legs onto the bed, he stirred, but didn't wake up. I'll let him sleep for another hour. The delivery truck is supposed to be here about ten, I'll get him up before then.

It was getting to be a warm sunny day, she opened the kitchen window and a cool, soft breeze came through it. The kitchen curtains moved slowly with the breeze. She filled the coffee maker, turned it on and went upstairs. She showered, dressed and came back downstairs. She had cereal for breakfast. At nine she went up to the bedroom and shook Chris gently.

"The delivery truck will be here in about an hour."

He opened his eyes slowly. "Ok, I'd better get up."

After doing his morning ritual, he came down stairs.

"I had cereal, do you want some?"

"Sure, that'll be fine, but I'd like a cup of coffee, do you want another one?"

"Ok," she said as he filled her cup then poured himself a cup. After a few sips he got up, got a bowl, spoon, milk and the cereal. Twenty minutes later a delivery truck pulled up in front of the house. Jennifer looked out the window when she heard the truck. "It's the delivery truck, the door's here."

Chris went outside just as the driver was getting out of the truck. The driver asked if he was Chris Manlee, Chris acknowledged 'yes'. He had a delivery for him, where did he want it. Chris told him and pointed to place it beside the wall with the man door. The driver asked him to sign the receipt, he did, and was given a copy.

The driver commented, "Be careful when you install the spring, it can be dangerous."

"Ok," said Chris, "I'm just going to repair the damaged panels not the spring."

"Looks like quite the damage, what happened?"

"Backed into them."

"Well, if the frame didn't get bent, it should be an easy job to replace the panels. Backing into the door can cause a lot of damage - they're not very strong, sure is a big hole, almost looks like somebody torched it."

Chris responded to the remark saying he had a busy day ahead. The driver called his helper who was standing beside the truck. After a short while the door, consisting of five wrapped panels, a long piece of narrow steel and a large box were unloaded. The driver reminded Chris that if he wanted he could get some people from the shop to install the door.

"I'll try it myself." Chris was getting annoyed both the driver and the sales clerk tried to get him to hire their company to fix the door. He told them that if he has a problem he'll call. They got into the truck, the driver leaned out the window and said, "good luck, if you need help just call us."

"Thanks," replied Chris as they drove away.

Chris walked over to look at the new door parts, and heard the phone ring in the distance. Jennifer yelled to Chris that it was High Tech Security Supplies calling and Chris's parts for the security system were in. She asked him if he was going to pick them up or does he want them delivered. Have them delivered was his response. The supply company said they could and the parts would be there in the afternoon. Chris opened the box to see the door parts - there were bolts, nuts and hinges. Ten minutes later there was another phone call. Jennifer answered the phone and it was Rich. He asked if Chris got his email and she said he hadn't checked it yet, but would he like to talk to him.

"Yes, is he close by?"

"Just a minute, I'll get him. Chris, your brother's on the phone," she yelled out the window.

"Be right in," as he hurried to the phone.

Jennifer put her hand over the phone's mouthpiece and said softly to Chris, "don't tell him yet everything that's happened."

He shook his head in agreement.

"Rich, how are you doing, did you find out about the insulator?"

"Yes, I sent you an email this morning, guess you haven't checked your email yet."

"No, I had a door delivered, the truck just left so I haven't had a chance."

"Ok, the insulator company is making some extremely good ones, even our company is starting to use them now."

"There's a model even better than the 135, it's the 150 and they have them in stock, they're sending you one for free."

"That's great, when is it being sent?"

"By courier today, should have it tomorrow."

"Thanks for your help."

"Hey, what are brothers for?"

"We'll keep you informed of what is happening."

"Would still like to go on one of the time trips, maybe Jennifer, Donna, John, you and I?"

"We will definitely have to plan for a trip once everything is back to normal, see you later."

"Have to go check the email," he said walking to the bedroom on the main level.

"Did he find one?"

"Yes"

Chris turned on the computer and in a few minutes the screen came up with all the icons. He clicked the mouse on the email icon and about twenty emails appeared on the screen. Jennifer walked in as the email from Rich opened.

HELLO CHRIS,

GOOD NEWS.

THE INSULATOR YOU WERE LOOKING FOR IS AVAILABLE EVEN IN A BETTER MODEL CALLED THE 150. IT'S A LOT LIGHTER THAN THE REGULAR INSULATORS, MADE OF SOME FORM OF POROUS MATERIAL, THEN SEALED TO KEEP OUT MOISTURE.

THEY DON'T SELL DIRECT, BUT I PHONED AND THEY ARE SENDING YOU ONE.

NO CHARGE.

I TOLD THEM YOU WERE DOING SOME EXPERIMENTING WITH HIGH VOLTAGE.

IT'S COMING BY COURIER.

YOU'LL HAVE IT TOMORROW.

BEST TO YOU AND JENNIFER,

RICH.

Chris replied to the email.

THANKS.

SHOULD SOLVE THE PROBLEM.

THE LAST ONE ALMOST DID.

BEST TO YOU, DONNA AND JOHN,

CHRIS AND JENNIFER.

He moved the mouse and clicked 'SEND'. Jennifer asked if it was the insulator he needed. It looks very promising, and could solve the problem he advised.

He went outside and started taking the wrapping off the panels. Another delivery truck came down the driveway to the TS building where Chris was standing. The driver got out of the truck and asked if he was Chris Manlee. Chris replied 'Yes'. He had a delivery from High Tech Security Supplies for him and asked him to sign a receipt. He signed the slip and the driver gave him a copy. Chris told the driver to place it beside the man door next to the panels. The driver made two trips placing the two boxes beside the panels. He commented on the size of the garage and asked if he 'worked on his own cars'. Chris thought for a few seconds and said it was his hobby. He asked what happened to the door.

"Looks like a lot of damage on that door, almost like someone took a torch to it."

"I backed into it with a winch on a truck," was the only thing Chris could think of saying, "I don't think it will be tough to repair."

"Watch out for the spring on the door as they can be dangerous."

"Thanks for delivering the parcel."

"No problem," he said as he got into the delivery truck and drove off.

Everybody seems to be an expert on garage doors he thought. He unpacked the panels, carried them over to the roll up door, went inside and removed the wood covering the hole.

This shouldn't be too hard, he thought, but could be a while to take the old bolts and hinges off and replace them. Everything went fine until the third panel, he had trouble holding it in place and bolting it at the same time. He called to Jennifer to come and help him to hold the panel on the door frame while he bolted them.

She barely heard him but replied, "Ok, be right out."

In about an hour the new panels were on.

"Thanks, for your help. The top ones were really difficult."

"Ok", she said, and was going to phone her mom and dad to find out how they were doing in Florida – she hadn't talked to them in a long time. Chris told her to give them his regards and also to her sister. She went to the house while Chris piled the old panels behind the building. A half hour later he went into the house and sat at the kitchen table.

"Glad that's done, next is the security system ...... I'll install it when we get back. How's your mom and dad? Was Ashley there?"

"They're fine, still asking when we're coming for a visit. Ashley wasn't there, she's at some function at the University."

Chris changed the subject........

"I've been thinking about how to solve the Nick and Mike/Geoff situation."

They should first get Nick, return him to 2104, pick up the suits and portable travel devices. Next they could pick up some stun guns and make a return trip to get Mike and Geoff. Maybe 'buy them off' or another option of moving to another state and not let anyone, except their families know where they went. They would have to move before they got Mike and Geoff.

"What about asking Nick if he could help us, he's a police officer; they could be in jail because of the disturbance," said Jennifer.

"They probably don't have much money and that could be a big problem for them, on the other hand, we might have to get them out of jail.," replied Chris.

They decided to first get Nick back and see if he could help them, if not, option two was to move. Where to move was the question - California, Texas, Arizona, what about Florida?

"Well I guess we'll find out what can be done after I get the insulator installed tomorrow."

How were they to find Nick? Perhaps try and find an address or phone number for the Bronos. That evening they went out for dinner, and lingered quite long talking more about the trip.

"Might need some more money in seventy two," said Chris.

"Why don't you go to the coin store and get about fifteen coins?"

"Why do we need that many?"

"Not sure, but we should be prepared. Tracking him down could be expensive if he's in a jail or hospital."

"Ok, with the five we have left, that'll give us plenty."

CHAPTER 22

The next morning at 7:00 am the alarm rang. After breakfast Chris worked on the TS, doing some checking on the control modules. Around 11:00 am, a delivery truck pulled up to the house. The driver went to the door and rang the doorbell. Jennifer went to the door. The delivery was from the insulator company. She signed the receipt and the driver handed her the parcel, went back to his truck and drove off. The parcel wasn't heavy so she carried it out to Chris. He opened it. The insulator was much shorter and wider. The box contained information on the insulator, double the rating of the old one in the TS. Jennifer hoped it worked solving the problem once and for all.

He'd have to do some modifications, some cable lengths and the mounting position needed to be adjusted. He had it all done by 3:10 in the afternoon, ready for testing. Testing was done later that afternoon.

Chris went into the house, all excited, "tested and works perfectly, were ready to go."

"Ok" said Jennifer, "I'll get the extra coins and be back within an hour."

"We'll be ready to leave when you get back."

Jennifer went to the coin store, got the coins and returned.

"I'll pack a few things, we might be there overnight," she said.

"Good idea," said Chris. "Don't forget my shaving stuff."

"Will do," she said, "and some clean clothes."

Fifteen minutes later she walked into the TS building with a small bag and put it on the back seat of the TS. Chris was already sitting in the TS with the date set to Tuesday, May 17, 2072, 10 am.

"Get in and close the door – we're all set."

She got into the TS, closed the door and Chris pressed the button and moved the switch. They were on their way to 2072. The surroundings changed along with the weather. This time the TS sounded great – no arching and the initial time acceleration and travel were very smooth. At the destination, the weather was cloudy and a light rain was falling.

"We have to go to the coin shop and get some money," said Jennifer.

Chris started the TS and drove to the city.

"Go directly to the parking garage," said Jennifer, "I don't know what would happen if we got stopped with seventy year old plates."

The parking garage was the same as in 2104 but the display was different than the one in 2104. It showed all the parking spots available, so there was a choice, rather than being assigned one.

He pressed 16A and drove there.

"Take five of the coins, that should be more than enough for what we need."

"Ok," said Jennifer as she put the remainder in the glove box. "Give me the keys and I'll lock it."

Chris took the key out of the ignition. Jennifer put the coins in the glove box, locked it and gave the keys back to him. She got out and walked to the back of the TS. Chris used the remote control. 'Beep, beep', the lights flashed twice, the TS was locked. They walked down the ramp and to the coin store. The stores had familiar names, but didn't have quite the same type of displays as in 2104. Some were holographic, but not to the extent of what they saw further into the future. Eventually they got to the coin store.

"Let's only get three changed."

"Why," said Chris.

"If we need more, we'll come back.

"Well ...... ok."

They got two thousand, fifty seven dollars and twenty five cents for the three coins. There wasn't an option for a money card so they took the cash and left. The number of bills was not extensive; three of the bills were the new 'five hundreds'. As they left the store, Jennifer kept two of the 'five hundreds' and gave Chris the rest of the money.

"You know, it's interesting how the value of gold coins fluctuates in value regardless of the time," said Chris. "I'm hungry, let's get a newspaper and go eat," he added.

"Where do you want to go?"

"There's a café across from the parking garage, it looked ok from the outside and there's a news stand next to it."

Chris paid for the paper and they went into the café, ordered a sandwich and lemonade each. Chris looked at the front page.

'MOON STATION TO BE A PERMANENT JOINT VENTURE'

'WILL HELP FOR MARS EXPLORATION'

He read the article..........................

"In 2060 there were five countries, United States, Russia, European Union, China and Japan with Moon bases. An agreement was signed, linking all sites by tunnels, making a small city on the moon. The same is planned for Mars after the bases are established. It is expected to be partially operational by 2098 with the moon serving as a supply site for the trips. Dynoelectromagnetic pulsed drives developed a decade ago, have contributed greatly to the settling of the moon but Super Dynoelectromagnetic drives, under development are expected to be useable within ten years."

"Thought Dynoelectromagnetic drives were only theory," said Chris.

"Looks like they've developed them, the theory was proposed many years ago."

He looked at the paper and continued, "With a combined moon base the exploration of Mars would be more extensive. They found skeletal remains of a human in the ice in 2035 on the first Manned Mars trip. It goes on to say that they plan to start in an area that possibly had a city because they found stone columns under the ice. If a way is found to vaporize the ice, Mars could be green again by creating a livable atmosphere. A lot has sure happened in the last 100 years."

"Is there anything about Nick in there?"

"Here's something, a man on a school bus with a gun."

"Nick could have materialized inside a school bus," said Jennifer.

Chris summarized the story.......................

"He appeared in a school bus according to the driver and the eight year old passengers. The kids weren't hurt. The man was arrested later at his home and has a bail hearing pending. It's Nick!"

"He can get from two to ten years in jail if convicted for a weapons possession on a school bus. It says here he claims to be a policeman from the future."

"Hope they don't take him seriously, that could make it difficult to rescue him," said Jennifer.

"We'll have to go to the bail hearing and get him released."

"And return him to his own time," added Jennifer.

"We should go visit him and explain what we're planning to do."

"Could be tricky - what if we're asked how we know him?"

"Ok, we'll go to the hearing, then see what we can do."

"There's another way, phone his family, maybe they can help."

"Good idea, we'll use a pay phone so it's not traceable," said Chris. "Let's find a hotel first, then phone," said Jennifer.

They finished eating. Outside they could see signs for two hotels protruding above the buildings.

"Let's try that one," said Chris pointing to the closest one, "must be just around the corner."

They went to the parking lot, got the bag and walked to the hotel. It was old, but clean and had a large lobby area with chairs and a sofa. A family of four was at one end. A boy and girl about 5 and 7 years old were playing quietly. The kids glanced at them and waved. They smiled and waved back.

Hotel employees were dressed in blue uniforms with a gold stripe down the legs. At the front desk they were greeted by, 'hello, welcome to Universal Imperial Towers Hotel, can I help you?' Chris asked if they had a room for one night. The clerk asked if they had a reservation and Chris responded 'no'. The hotel had rooms. The price was one hundred and seventy six dollars for one night. They asked for two entry cards.

"Just a moment and I'll get the guest form. We can run your credit card through for an imprint."

"Can we pay cash?"

"Yes"

A screen about a foot square was in the desktop.

He placed a slip on a screen and said. "Please fill in your name and address then sign the bottom."

Chris filled out the form and gave the address that they were living at in 2004 along with their phone number. He paid the desk clerk and picked up the bag. The clerk handed him two entry cards and noted that the room was paid on the form.

The room was 202. If they wanted something to eat, the restaurant was open from 7 am to 10 pm and check out time was 2 pm. They took the elevator to the second floor.

At room 202, Chris set the bag down and placed the entry card on, 'PLACE ENTRY CARD HERE AND PRESS ENTER'

'IF YOU TRY TO ACCESS THIS ROOM WITH AN INVALID KEY AN ALARM WILL SOUND AT THE FRONT DESK.'

He pressed 'ENTER' and the door opened.

The room was about the same size as their bedroom at home. Inside a cabinet with glass doors was something that looked like a TV, but without a screen. It had some sort of projection device on it. There was a label on the front of it. 'VV MODEL 5023' 'MULTI SIZE SCREEN DISPLAY'

Chris put the bag on the bed and Jennifer began unpacking it. He picked up the remote control from the night table, pointed it at the VV and pressed 'ON'. A picture was projected in front of the cabinet, in the air, similar in size to a 19 inch TV.

"Look at this," said Chris.

Jennifer came out of the bathroom where she had placed the toothpaste, brushes and shaving supplies.

"That's different," she said.

Chris looked at the remote control and saw a joy stick labeled "SCREEN SIZE AND POSITION." Pressing it to the right, the screen increased to three feet. Pressing down, it tilted down. The sound came from all over the room, not loud and blasting but quiet and clear. 'Wow," said Chris, "TV technology has sure advanced."

"We should look for the Brono's phone number."

"Ok, where's the phone book?" asked Chris, as he shut the VV off.

Jennifer walked over to the telephone that was on a desk at the far end of the room. It had a small screen displaying the Numbers at the top and the letters just below it.

'PRESS HERE FOR VIDEO COMMUNICATION AND REMAIN WITHIN 160 DEGREES OF THE CAMERA.'

"The phones are video," she said. "We'll have to be careful when we phone the Bronos, the camera operates at one hundred and sixty degrees."

"Can we cover the camera up?"

"Don't think we can, if the camera is covered, the phone won't work."

"We'll think of something."

"Have you seen a phone book anywhere in the room?" asked Jennifer.

"Haven't, there's probably one in a drawer."

Looking in all the drawers, they couldn't find one. Jennifer called the front desk for a phone book. The clerk told her they didn't have phone books and to press 'PHONE NUMBERS' on the phone screen and follow the directions.

"Thanks," she said and hung up. "No phone books, we get them through the screen menu."

She pressed 'PHONE NUMBERS', a menu appeared with enter 'STATE, CITY, NAME, ADDRESS.'

She entered the data without the address. Pressing a key labeled 'FIND', the display came up with 'Brono, James at 1595 Washington Road and a Brono, Carey at 1233 Sunnyside Drive.'

"There's two Bronos, one on Washington Road, the other on Sunnyside Drive."

"Write down both the numbers."

Jennifer pressed the one for James.

'P17-503-555-1734.'

'WOULD YOU LIKE THIS NUMBER DIALED?"

Writing the number on a pad, next to the phone she pressed 'NO'. She pressed the one for Carey.

'P17-503-555-1212.'

"WOULD YOU LIKE THIS NUMBER DIALED?"

Writing the number pressing 'NO'.

Turning to Chris "I have phone numbers, shall we try them?"

"There's a phone booth just outside the hotel, lets try that one," Chris said.

Jennifer went inside and read the instructions while Chris stood outside the phone both with the door open. On the screen was 'VIDEO DISABLE'. She pressed it. The phone, similar to the one in the hotel room, had the numeric and alphabet keypads.

'LOCAL PHONE CALLS - ONE DOLLAR'

Depositing a dollar Jennifer dialed the number listed for Jim.

'Ring.........', 'ring.........', and a male voice said "Hello."

"Hello, we're inquiring if you know a person by the name of Nick Brono?"

"Who's calling, turn on the video."

"We're friends of Nick."

"There's a Nick here, he's three years old – are you talking about the other Nick?"

"Yes, Nick in the paper, we can help him, we're sort of the reason he is in trouble."

"Are you the ones involved with this future thing?"

"Can we meet and talk?" asked Jennifer.

"Don't know - the story he told was hard to believe."

"Let's meet; we can return him back to 2104."

After hearing the year, Jim thought, 'That's the year Nick mentioned.' "Ok, where?" he said.

"Can we meet at your home?"

"Ok, at 7:00 tonight, do you have a way to get here and the address?"

"Yes, but give me your address just to make sure."

"1595 Washington Road, do you know how to get here?"

She repeated the address; they had a map and would be there at seven.

She heard a 'click' then hung up the phone.

"I know where that is," said Chris, "it's the area they started to develop in the early nineties, just a few miles across the main road from our house."

They walked to the TS and drove to the exit.

"Got the parking ticket?"

"Yes," said Jennifer as she got it from behind the sun visor on her side. They paid for the parking, drove directly to Washington Road and parked on the street. They walked up the driveway. At the front door Chris pressed the doorbell.

Jim opened the door about a foot.

"Are you the people that phoned?"

"Yes," said Jennifer.

"Come in."

They went in. Tania was sitting on a couch, Adam wasn't there. Jim introduced Tania to Chris and Jennifer. Chris and Jennifer introduced themselves (first name only) to Jim and Tania. Tania asked if Nick was from the future as he claimed.

"Yes, and we're here to help him get back," said Chris.

"How're you going to do that, he's in jail," said Jim.

"We could get him out on bail," said Jennifer.

"Could be expensive, we don't have the money for bail," said Jim.

"That's where we can help, let's wait and see how much it is," said Chris.

Jim asked Chris if they knew where the hearing was and when. He told them it was at 10:00 the next morning at the County court house. They agreed to meet there at 9:30 the next morning. Tania, quiet for most of the time, asked about the spark that went between the two Nicks.

"When their hands got close there was a big spark, almost like a small lightning bolt, between them ......, was that static electricity?"

"Don't think so, must be that two of the same objects cannot occupy the same space at the same time ... its theoretical physics. When they came together the space they occupied could not be the same, don't let them come close or touch each other, there could be some serious problems."

Tania asked her how she knew that and Jennifer replied that she was a physicist. They continued talking and Chris explained what happened and how Nick got there. Jim asked where they got a time traveling machine and Chris explained that they built it. Jim was impressed, but didn't say anything. It was past eight o'clock.

"We've taken enough of your time," said Jennifer, "We gotta go."

"Do you know how to get to the court house?" Jim asked.

"No, what's the direction."

Jim explained the directions and they left after agreeing to meet the next morning. They drove to the parking garage. After parking the TS and locking it – beep, beep

– lights flash, Chris suggested they go to the restaurant in the hotel to which Jennifer agreed because it was getting late. The restaurant wasn't crowded, just four tables were being used.

"Would you like to have dinner," asked a young lady at the entrance.

"Yes," replied Jennifer.

They followed her to a table set for two near the center of the room. Jennifer ordered wine and Chris a beer. She told them the menu was located to the right just under the tabletop. They reached under the table and removed a device that looked like a hand computer, about six inches square, a half-inch thick. The screen displayed the restaurant name and on the touch screen there was "PRESS HERE FOR MENU".

They pressed menu – the restaurant's menu was displayed. The waitress told them to scroll down the menu and when they got to something they liked, touch the screen ...... it'll be displayed ... and to order press the order button.

"Quite the menus," Chris said.

"I think I'll see how the salmon looks," said Jennifer.

She touched the Salmon button. The screen displayed a short video and description of the meal.

"This is great to see what the meals looks like."

Chris pressed the 'New York Steak' and the video came on.

"Check the salmon," said Jennifer.

Chris pressed the salmon on the menu and the video came on.

"Looks good, that's what I'm ordering," he said.

"I think I will too."

They selected the Salmon by pressing 'ORDER'.

"DO YOU WANT SEPARATE CHECKS?"

Chris pressed 'NO'.

'WHICH MENU DO YOU WANT THE BILL TO?' Chris's menu had a '2' on it, so he pressed 2.

'SELECT THE TYPE OF POTATOES, VEGETABLES AND SALAD.' They made their selection.

'YOUR SALAD WILL BE BROUGHT TO YOU IN 5 MINUTES.

THE SALMON WILL BE BROUGHT TO YOU IN 27 MINUTES.

TO ORDER ADDITIONAL REFRESHMENTS GO TO THE REFRESHMENTS MENU.'

A few minutes later they had their drinks and the waitress asked if there was anything else she could get them.

"No, everything is just fine," Jennifer said.

An hour later they were finished dinner. The waitress came to the table, "anything else you'd like?"

"No" Chris replied, "can we have our check?"

"The amount is displayed on the menu .... just press "'All' then 'total' and follow the directions. Place your credit card on the screen when you're done."

"We'd like to pay cash."

"Press the cash button and a bill will be printed out the bottom of the menu. You can pay at the receptionist's counter on the way out."

Chris followed the instruction, include a tip and a check was printed. They walked to the desk, paid and went to their room.

Sitting on the bed, Chris grabbed the remote and said, "Want to watch some TV?"

"I think I'll check out the paper - where is it?"

"It's on the chair in the corner."

Jennifer got the newspaper, sat in the chair and began to read. Chris turned on the TV (VV) and the late news was on. The remote had another group of buttons labeled sound. The sound could be directed to one person watching the VV by moving the button to the left, the sound started to become directional. Moving the button up, the sound moved in his direction.

"You can turn it up if you want," Jennifer said as she looked up from reading the paper.

Chris thought it was great, the sound was coming directly at him and wasn't reflecting throughout the room. He told her to come and hear it. She walked over but couldn't hear any sound until she got beside Chris.

"This is great, you can watch TV, not disturbing anyone."

She went back to the chair and newspaper. The news came on and the TV announcer started to talk about the Moon base.

"The moon base will be connected by tunnels."

An animation came on to show how they would be connected.

"Machines with laser bits will bore holes between the complexes and vaporize the moon rock creating a glazed tunnel. The advantage is no debris to remove but they're still working on a method to remove the vapors. The problem is that there's no atmosphere on the moon, a solution should be forthcoming within a year."

A commercial came on.

"That's progress," said Chris.

"What's that?"

"They were talking about the Moon base of interconnecting tunnels."

After the commercial the announcer talked about Mars. "More planned trips and exploration of Mars are planned ...... the finding of a body that looks human just under the ice, has created enthusiasm by world governments to explore Mars."

A picture came on showing what looked like a person lying on their side in a green robe. The face wasn't visible.

"Come and see this." Chris said.

"What is it?"

"It's a picture of what's thought to be a human frozen on Mars."

She looked over to the TV but the picture had changed to the next story.

"What did it say?"

"Just that they wanted to speed up the exploration, anything interesting in the paper?"

"No, just the regular stuff, the ads are interesting."

"This ad for a TV, or as they call them VVs, has a three meter (10 ft) screen giving the effect of being in a theater."

"Another ad has VV glasses, you can watch TV with the effect of being in a theater with full sound."

Jennifer looked at the clock beside the bed, it was 10:47 pm. They set the alarm clock for 7:00 am. Tomorrow would be a demanding day – would they be able to get Nick released? Would Nick help them with the Mike and Geoff problem?

CHAPTER 23

May 18, 2072. Buz..............zzz. Jennifer reached over, looked at the clock and pressed 'snooze' on the alarm clock. She rubbed her eyes and laid there for a few minutes, then slowly sat up in bed. Chris rolled onto his back, opened his eyes, yawned, and then stretched. Jennifer turned the alarm off and got out of bed. "Come on, Chris, better get out of bed and get ready, it's 7:00 am."

"O ...... k,' with another yawn, "slept like a rock," as he sat up and put his feet on the floor.

"So did I," as she walked to the bathroom.

In an hour they were ready to go down for breakfast. The hotel restaurant was crowded, only a few tables left. Some people at the tables were reading the newspaper. The waitress asked if they wanted breakfast. Jennifer said 'yes' and were taken to a table. After being seated they ordered coffee. No directions needed this time for the menus. Pressing 'BREAKFAST', there was a display of the meals. The waitress returned with a coffee pot, a bowl of sugar, a small pitcher of cream and set them on the table. She poured the coffee.

They both ordered hot cakes.

'YOUR ORDER WILL BE DELIVERED IN 14 MINUTES' was displayed on the screen.

The waitress brought their orders and set them on the table. They ate and talked, mostly hoping that everything would work out. The clock on the menu screen displayed a few minutes before nine. After they finished they went through the routine of getting their bill and paid it on the way out.

It was 9:40 am when they got to the courthouse. Jim and Adam were standing on the steps outside the courthouse.

"Hello, everything set," said Chris.

Jim introduced them. They shook hands and Adam asked if they were the future people.

"We're actually from the past," said Jennifer.

"Quiet Adam," Jim said, "it's going to be enough of a problem to get Nick released, we don't need anybody hearing that."

Jim asked them if they were going inside. No, because they didn't want Nick to see them yet. They'd wait outside. Chris got a newspaper and they sat on one of the benches in the lobby reading.

Jim and Adam went into the courtroom, sat down and waited for Nick's hearing. At 10:12 am there was an announcement to bring out Nick Brono.

Nick walked in with one guard and the attorney that had been assigned to him. The case was read as the state versus Nick Brono. The judge asked the defendant and attorney to stand and the charges were read. A plea was read and the attorney replied not guilty based on no violence or harm done. The judge disagreed, set a trial date and bail for ten thousand dollars. The attorney thanked the judge. Nick looked back and saw Jim and Adam.

Adam gave the thumbs up sign and said silently, "will get your bail." Nick smiled.

After Nick was removed from the courtroom, they went to Chris and Jennifer and told them bail was ten thousand dollars.

"We can get that amount," Chris said as he looked at Jim.

"We only need ten percent and that comes to a thousand dollars," said Adam.

"Yes, but if you put up bail and he doesn't show up, you'll have to pay the balance," said Jennifer.

"Ok, what do we do now?" asked Jim.

Chris and Jennifer would get the money and meet them back here at 1:00 o'clock. Jim would do the work to get Nick out. Walking to the hotel, Jennifer suggested they check out and put their things in the TS. They walked to the TS, put the bag on the back seat and opened the glove box. There were fifteen coins in the glove box.

"We got six hundred and eighty dollars for each before," said Jennifer, "should need about fifteen to get ten thousand dollars,"

They walked to the coin store and up to the counter.

"We'd like to change these coins for cash," as she handed the clerk fifteen coins. They were worth ten thousand two hundred and seventeen dollars and twenty-five cents. The clerk asked if she wanted a check.

No, she wanted cash. He had to check to see if they had enough cash and returned - they would have to be in five hundred dollar bills. Jennifer said that five hundreds would be fine. After counting the money he handed her an envelope with $10,000 in it and another with the balance of the money. She put them in her pocket and they left the store. It was 11:50 am.

"Want something to eat before we go back?" There was a burger place next door.

"Ok!"

The place was quite busy. Most of the people were teenagers while some looked like office workers because of their clothes. A booth near the back was empty so they sat there. They ordered burgers and lemonade. Twenty minutes later they were finished.

"Better get going, it's twenty past twelve," said Jennifer.

They got to the courthouse just before 1:00 o'clock; Jim and Adam weren't there but showed up at 1:05 pm.

"Did you get the money?" Jim asked.

"Yes, how do we do this," she said.

Jim would set up a bank account and give a thousand dollars deposit, but would need nine thousand collateral. If Nick didn't show up for the trial, which he wasn't going to, the remainder would have to be surrendered.

Jennifer got the envelope containing $10,000 out of her pocket and gave it to Jim. He put the envelope in his jacket pocket and went across the street to a bank to set up an account while Chris, Jennifer and Adam waited outside the courthouse.

At the counter, he asked to set up a checking account. He was given options and selected a standard one and asked when the funds would be available. For cash - immediately. He filled out the application, smiling as he gave the clerk the money. The clerk brought the checks over, and welcomed Jim as a bank customer.

In the meantime Jennifer had walked over to the bank door, peeked in occasionally and signaled back to Chris and Adam with a 'thumbs up' that everything was ok. The whole procedure took about twenty minutes. Jennifer and Jim walked back to the courthouse. They moved away from the front door to discuss the next step. Jim went to the information desk to ask the guard where to go to post bail. The bail office was in Room 122. An elderly lady was the clerk at the bail office. He said he wanted to post bail for Nick Brono. She went to a computer and came back with a few questions.

"Are you related to Nick Brono?"

He thought quickly and said. "He's .... my brother."

She asked for ID and he showed her his driver's license.

"Oh, I remember this one; he was the one that said he was from the future."

Referring to Nick, Jim said, "he reads a lot, scifi stories – you know how those people are."

She gave no response to that comment.

"Ok, you will need a check for one thousand dollars and collateral for the remaining nine thousand," she said.

"I have a bank account, can I use that?"

"You can if you have nine thousand dollars available – it'll be frozen until he comes to trial and if he is a 'no show', you forfeit all nine thousand plus the thousand you give me today."

"That's fine, I'll make sure he'll be at the trial."

"Fill out this form, sign it that you will be responsible for him to appear in court on the proper date and if he fails you will relinquish all the bail monies."

Jim filled out the form, signed it and gave it to her. She handed him another form and told him he would have to get it filled out at the bank and authorized for the assignment. He walked out, near the entrance were Chris, Jennifer and Adam. He told them he had to get a form authorized at the bank.

Jim went to the bank. At the service counter he asked to see a bank officer to get a form authorized. The receptionist called one on the phone. A man greeted him and asked what he could do for him. Jim explained what he needed and the man filled out the form, authorized it and gave it back to him. Jim walked back to the courthouse where Chris, Jennifer and Adam were standing outside. He went back to room 122 and handed the form to the clerk along with a check.

She printed a release form and told him to take it to the county detention center where Nick would be released into his custody. It was open from 9 am to 5 pm and the time was after 3:00 pm. Jim left the office and made arrangements with Chris and Jennifer to meet him at his place at 7:00 o'clock that evening. Jim and Adam left to get Nick.

Walking back Jennifer said, "what are we going to do for three hours?"

"We'll go to the TS, go back home and wait there until 6:30 tonight."

They went to the parking lot, paid for parking and drove the TS to their home. The drive took longer than normal as it was rush hour.

It was about 4:20 before Jim and Adam reached the county detention center. They gave the forms to the guard and in twenty minutes Nick came out dressed in his police uniform. In his hand was his jacket and all his belongings except the gun. They told Nick about Chris and Jennifer. He was mad and glad, mad they got him into this situation but glad they were going to get him back. The plan was for 7:00 o'clock that evening, when they would pick him up for the time travel.

"Remember to stay away from small Nick, there could be big problems if you two get too close."

"Ok, I know, that was sure painful when the spark went between us."

At 7:00 pm Jennifer and Chris pulled up to the Brono house.

They walked up the driveway to the front door.

Ring………, they rang the doorbell once.

Jim opened the door. Adam and Nick were sitting together with little Nick on Tania's lap and Nick sitting across the room.

'Meet Chris and Jennifer," said Jim.

"I don't know if this is good or bad - I wouldn't be in this situation if it weren't for your time traveling machine."

"We didn't mean for this to happen," said Chris. "We can't go directly back to 2104, the time traveling machine only works on one travel, from our home in 2004 to the destination, then back to 2004."

"You mean I have to go further into the past?"

"Yes, to get back to your home time."

"Well, I guess I haven't anything to lose, when can we go?"

"Right now," said Chris.

Nick got his jacket - everything was still wrapped in it.

"Well, Jim it was interesting knowing my father when he was young. Thanks for your help."

"Glad to be of help – to my son!" replied Jim.

"Mom, its strange calling you that, 'cause you are much younger than I am, I'm not going to get close - I don't want to hurt myself or little Nick - you know what I mean."

"Adam it was nice to see you, don't go to the conflict in seventy five, you could get seriously hurt."

"What do you mean?" questioned Adam.

"Just don't go - bye, bye little Nick." Strange feeling saying goodbye to yourself Nick thought.

He turned to Jennifer and Chris. "Ready to go"

"It was very nice meeting all of you, best of luck in the future."

Just as they were going out the door, Jim said. "Never did get your last name."

"Manlee," Chris said as they walked out the door.

Jennifer, Chris and Nick went to the TS. Driving to the old Manlee place, it didn't take long for them to become friends once Nick realized that they were trying to help him.

"We're going to need your help in twenty one 'O' four. The two people who stole this SUV will need to be brought back to our time in two thousand and four, we can't leave them there," said Chris.

"Do you want to bring them to justice?"

"No, we want to bring them back, it will be a problem because they know of this time traveling machine. How do we stop them from telling anyone when we get them back to our time?"

"There is a way to do it," said Nick. "There's a method of erasing a person's memory and putting something else in that spot, it's called a Memory Minder or MM."

"We've been using it for trauma victims so they don't have to remember terrible events."

As they drove a police patrol car came up behind them with the lights flashing.

"Wonder what he wants," said Chris.

"We're just about home, I'll start the time travel."

He set the date for August 31, 2004 at 10 pm, stopped and pressed the return button, then moved the switch for time travel. The officer just got out of his car and was walking up to the TS. A blue light came out of the back. The officer stood back wondering what was going on. The TS faded until it disappeared. They were on their way to 2004.

The police officer looked around, couldn't see anything then on the radio said, "the previous call for an ID - cancel it."

The TS started through the seasonal and day/night changes.

"This is fantastic, how come all this is happening, I went through the same thing when I was on the outside."

Chris turned to Nick. "It's just time speeding past us."

The insulator is working well - can't hear any sparking," said Chris as he turned to Jennifer.

As the TS approached 2004 it started to become transparent and floated through the wall, turned and settled in its landing spot.

"That was quite a trip," said Nick, "but it seemed short."

"It's shorter because the TS is working properly now, when you were holding onto the TS, there was a malfunction in the insulator that caused it to slow down.

I guess it's not funny, but you sure had a strange look on your face when you were on the outside."

"I didn't know what was going on."

They got out of the TS, Nick grabbed his jacket and everything in it. He set the jacket on the table beside the computers.

"When are we going to go to the future?"

"Have to check the insulator just to make sure it was ok, should be soon if we don't have any problems."

"I'll check it tomorrow, if it's ok we leave tomorrow."

"Anything I can do," said Nick.

"No, with all you've been through in the last few days, you deserve to just relax."

Chris turned to Jennifer, "would you like something to drink, Jennifer?"

"A glass of wine, but I'll go get it, I've got a few things to do."

He turned to Nick. "Want a beer?"

"Ok, don't know what kind you have, any type will do."

Chris went into the house and got a couple of beers. Back at the TS building he twisted the caps off the beers and gave one to Nick. Jennifer walked in with a glass of wine. "It's sure a lovely evening, let's go outside."

They walked out the man door; it was a clear, warm night with a full moon and many stars.

"Sure is nice around here from what I've seen," said Nick.

"Yes, we enjoy it, it's far enough out of the city - do you have a family back home, Nick?"

"Only my parents, which you met and a fiancé', her name is Camrela and she is a fantastic person."

“Are you getting married?”

“About two months – October 18th. She is probably wondering where I am.”

“Don’t worry about that, we’ll set the time to return a few hours after you left, she won’t even know you’ve been gone,” said Chris.

Just then the phone rang.

“I’ll get that,” said Jennifer, “wonder who’s calling so late?”

The phone was ringing a third time when Jennifer got to it.

It was Donna, she had phoned earlier in the evening but didn’t get an answer. “We just got back,” said Jennifer. They talked for a while longer and Jennifer told her some of what had happened. “The next time we get together I’ll explain it all to you.”

Chris and Nick were still outside, standing in the yard.

Chris turned to Nick. “Have you figured out how you’re going to tell your partner what happened?”

“I’ll have to give that some thought, the other problem is the communicator, utility pouch and the gun I don’t have.”

“I don’t know what time era my pouch landed in, the gun is still in ‘72.”

“Could do a search in 2104 in the police records and see if I could find out what happened to the gun, but I’ve got to have it when we go back or I’ll be in big trouble.”

“Losing all those things is going to be difficult to explain to the commander.”

“When we were driving you mentioned that there was a way of erasing a certain part of a person’s memory and replacing it with some other memory.”

"It's done by some of the memory specialists. We call them MS's. The doctors work on the memory part of the brain electronically and through some probes and a computing device change the memory. We call it an MM."

"That could help us with the two men, remember the ones banging on the windows."

"I do have a doc friend who does it, I might be able get him to help."

"What kind of equipment do they use, is it portable?"

"The new ones are portable. The doc's come to the police station sometimes but most of the time it's in the hospitals."

"There was a stun gun we saw that would knock someone out for about an hour."

"Oh, that's the 'demobilizing gun', you can get those at any sporting goods or gun store."

"We tried," said Chris, "they wanted a driver's permit and a police check, couldn't do that because our driver's permit would be a hundred years old and we wouldn't be in a police data base - we didn't exist in 2104."

"I can purchase one and help you bring them back, if the doc can't help," said Nick.

"We'll demobilize them, bring them here, if you can get your doctor friend to replace their memory that would be even better - by here I mean to this spot in twenty one 'O' four."

I might be able to get my partner to help us – I'll have to be careful on that approach because she might not believe me and think I'm off my rocker. I guess we'll find out when we get back there."

"Nick, if we're driving in the TS and our plates are 100 years old is there a chance we would get stopped by the police?"

"Not likely because it's an antique."

"You could have problems with the environmental police. They're dead against internal combustion engines because they caused pollution. The pollution has eased up quite a bit though 'cause cars using gasoline engines aren't produced anymore. Even oil is used very rarely. Anything needing a slippery surface is molecularly treated to have very low friction without oil. It was a new science that came out quite a few years ago called solids molecular engineering. It's a science, almost like a genetic engineering, for metals and other materials that changes the surface molecular structure for different characteristics including a slippery one."

Jennifer returned from talking on the phone.

"Who was that?" asked Chris.

"Donna, she was wondering how we were doing."

"Rich and her were worried about us and concerned about everything."

"Did you tell her that everything is ok?"

"Some, not everything, she said to phone them when everything is done."

"Will have to do that once we get Nick back and however we solve the Mike and Geoff situation."

"Ooo ...ps. forgot my wine in the house," as she turned and went back into the house. Chris turned to Nick. "I read in the paper that the Oxygen levels are increasing and the carbon dioxide levels are decreasing."

"Yes, that's what I meant about the environmental police and with no gas engines, the air pollution is gradually dispersing. Most of the heating including the industrial type is electrical coming from solar, plasma electric converters, and a form of fusion. Oh yes, also hydro electric is still used."

Jennifer returned with her wine.

"The article said it could cause reduced plant growth - with the reduction of carbon dioxide the temperatures could also drop a few degrees," said Chris.

"On TV or VV as you call it, there was a news story of a human found in the ice on Mars and a picture of it."

"Oh that, they finally dug him out and brought him back a few years ago, but didn't officially announce it - there's speculation that he's still in the ice. Rumors were that it was human, some reports had it as an alien and there were others that said it's just a hoax. I don't really know what's true. The first pictures were taken a long time ago."

"From what I saw on the VV it sure looked like a human figure."

"Rumor was that it's a doctored up picture."

They finished their beer. "Do you want another one?" Chris said.

"No thanks, one is all I can handle right now."

Jennifer said she was going to bed. "Nick, you can use the downstairs bedroom, Chris will show you where it is."

"Good night." She walked to the house.

Chris and Nick went to the TS. He took the cover off the insulator compartment; it was clean - no electrical tracking on it. "Finally got that problem solved," as he replaced the cover on the compartment. He checked the amount of energy used and hooked up the charging unit. The gauge showed that there was very little used but he wanted to have it fully charged.

"Looks like a complicated unit," said Nick.

"It took quite a few years to design but not much to build."

Chris turned the light off, locked the TS doors and the door to the TS building. Inside the house he showed Nick to the bedroom and bathroom. In the bathroom he opened a drawer.

"Here's a shaving kit, a packaged tooth brush is in the bottom drawer."

"Haven't used a razor much before, the first one I used was in seventy two and that was an experience, didn't cut myself though. They're difficult to get in 2104, almost all of the shavers have their own energy packs."

Chris nodded, and went upstairs to bed. There was planning to be done tomorrow on how they were going to get Nick's items back, especially the gun.

CHAPTER 24

September 1, 2004. It was just after 7:30 in the morning and Chris and Jennifer were awakening to another sunny warm day. They did their morning requirements and went downstairs. Nick had been up for over an hour, sitting on a chair in the porch with his feet up on a stool, just relaxing. He hadn't put the coffee on yet, as he didn't know how to use the coffee maker. Jennifer showed him how, making it at the same time. He was used to a fully automatic machine that measured the proper amount of coffee and water for the number of cups selected. After the first cup they had breakfast.

Chris and Jennifer were thrilled this morning as everything seemed to be turning out right. The TS was working properly with the new insulator and the roll up door was fixed. He still had to install the security system, but that could wait until everything was back to normal.

After breakfast Nick and Chris went to the porch and sat in the chairs.

"Nick, do you want to change from that uniform? You're about the same size as I am, you could wear some of my clothes."

"I'd like that, it'll be nice to get out of the uniform."

"What about your boots?"

"Oh, that's not a problem." He lifted a flap on the toe of the boot, pressed the 'DRESS SHOES' and the ankle high PATROL BOOTS' became shoes."

"I didn't even notice a flap there, how is that done - never thought of shoes having that type of feature?"

"The flap totally blends in with the boot, it's pretty slick how it's not noticeable. I don't know actually how it's done, all I do is press the button for one of the three settings, 'PATROL BOOTS, PURSUIT BOOTS OR DRESS. It saves having different types of boots and shoes for work or dress. I usually set them for patrol, which is normal when I'm working, but they can be changed to pursuit very fast. I should've changed them to shoes before but the patrol boots are the most comfortable."

"What kind of boot is for pursuit?" asked Chris.

"Now that's unique, in that form they give ankle and leg support and are very flexible. The sole of the boot has a springy composition to give a lift with each step, making it easier to run."

"Well, let's get you some 2004 clothes, come on."

They went upstairs and Chris got some jeans and a shirt, and handed them to Nick.

"Thanks, these look great." Nick changed the clothes and they went back to the porch and sat down.

"What type of work do you do?" Nick asked.

"I used to design computer chips, just have my, 'hobby' of the time traveling machine now."

Jennifer walked out to the deck and sat in the chair beside Chris.

"And what do you do, Jennifer?"

"I teach physics part time at the local college about nine months of the year. Even though it's not full time, it keeps me reasonably busy. Chris spends a lot of time on the TS so I also look after the orchard."

"Now that the TS is working properly, I'll have more time for other things," remarked Chris.

"Sounds like both of you are enjoying yourselves with the TS."

"It's been fun up 'til the 'break in', even though we didn't go on any trips before that. When it was stolen, everything changed."

"Why didn't you call the police?"

"Didn't want to explain about the TS, probably would have been some investigation. The TS could have been exposed, not that it's illegal."

"Good point, a sharp police officer probably would have noticed what was in there and had it further investigated."

It was 12:10 - past noon and Jennifer asked them if they would like some sandwiches. They said 'yes'. She asked if they would like a beer and both said 'yes'.

"The beer tastes better here than in my time, they use some method that makes the beer ready in a few days. Some sort of accelerated aging process they developed."

Chris asked him if he'd like to go to the city and see what it looked like. Nick was somewhat excited as they agreed to go after they ate, and wanted to see the Washington Road area also. That area was still under development and wouldn't be finished for another five years, but they could go and see what was happening there.

Jennifer brought out a tray with sandwiches, two beers and a glass of lemonade for herself. Both acknowledged her effort with a "thank you," to which she replied, "you're both welcome."

They reached for a sandwich and a beer. Chris turned to her. "We're going to the city, then over to Washington Road after lunch. Do you want to go?"

"I have some chores that should get done."

"Ok, we won't be long, probably a few hours."

After they ate, Chris and Nick got into the regular SUV (not the TS).

"Haven't been in a gasoline driven vehicle before, except for your time traveling machine. The only places I've seen these types of vehicles have been in the car museums or where someone has restored them. Not many places to get gasoline and it's over eight dollars a liter."

"When did they start using the metric system?"

"Was before my time, they still use the imperial system as there was never an official time for the conversion. With so many joint venture projects with other countries, especially in space, guess it just crept in."

Seeing that Chris was actually driving the SUV, he commented. "Do the cars have a guidance system for driving?"

"Not yet, there experimenting, but takes a lot of space – don't think it'll be out for a while - they had it in seventy two but it was much more improved in your time."

"The type in my time is great, the system doesn't need the magnetic blue lines. The new type uses standard road lines and monitors road conditions, should make accidents virtually non-existent. It's pretty slick the way it notifies and stops the car if there's a dangerous situation ahead."

"That's quite the technology, saw a demo in a car book from your time, in fact we have a book here. (He didn't want to mention about the other book Geoff and Mike's brought back - they had disabled it, anyway.) We don't have books with the features of your time, ours are still just paper."

"Hey, can we stop at a book store, I'd like to take a few back with me, they're collector's items."

"Ok, we can stop at the mall bookstore."

Chris turned into the mall, parked and headed for the bookstore.

"I don't have any money except my money card, would you mind if I got some money from you and paid you back in future?"

"Sure, but consider it a gift to you from our time to yours."

They went into the bookstore and Nick browsed the different books. His selection was a book on the 2004 cars and trucks, the other was a novel on a time travel written over a century ago.

"This book is still popular in my time, the copy I have is like watching a movie with sound but I prefer the story text running along the bottom, it's more like reading."

Chris paid for the books; they went back to the SUV and into the city.

Driving past the corner of Main and Statewide, Nick said, "This is the place where it happened, the buildings looked pretty much the same, not much advertising though. No billboard on the buildings and the stores don't have active displays, it's sort of nice this way."

"Those were quite the billboards with the advertising and holographic displays, how long have they been there?" asked Chris.

"Many years, as long as I can remember, they've changed over the years - got more active with holograms, almost interactive."

They drove through the city, while Nick pointed to familiar landmarks and commented about them.

"Like to see the house I grew up in, can we still go there?" asked Nick.

"Ok, don't know if it's even built – we can check it out, Washington Road is a short detour from our house."

"Sure appreciate that, it'll be interesting to see it new."

They drove back. Chris turned off at the exit and drove to where the house should be. The house was built and had a 'for sale' sign on it. The front door was open so they went inside where a lady realtor was sitting at a small desk.

"Are you the people who phoned about the house?"

"No just lookin'," said Nick, "whose coming over to see it?"

"Let me check here, it's a young couple named James and Bette Brono, do you know them?"

"Uh.........., no, just curious."

They turned away from the realtor and Nick said quietly to Chris, "they were my past relatives."

"Are you looking for a house to buy," she said.

"Not exactly, just browsing the area," said Nick.

A car drove up, out stepped a young couple. Walking into the house they saw Nick and Chris, but didn't pay attention to them.

"Are you the Brono's?"

"Yes," said James, "We'd like to see the house, are you busy – we could come back later."

Before she could answer, Nick said, "just leaving, a great house - will be fantastic for your children, and their decedents."

They looked at him puzzled, "thanks".

"What was that about?" Bette asked James.

"Haven't a clue what they're talking about."

Chris and Nick went to the SUV and drove away.

"I was tempted to tell them I was their relative, one of the greater ones. You remember my Uncle Adam?"

"Yes he's the one at Jim's house."

"He went to a conflict in seventy five, didn't come back, that's why I told him not to go in seventy five."

Chris thought Nick shouldn't have warned him of the situation …… guess the damage's been done, no sense mentioning it - I almost told my parents, guess I really can't blame him.

As they drove into the driveway, Chris said, "did you see much change?"

"The layout of the city is pretty much the same, many building fronts have changed including the advertising. Of course it's much smaller but otherwise looks the same."

Chris parked the SUV beside the house. There was a spot in the TS building for it, but they never parked it there. They got out of the SUV and walked to the house. It was just after 6:00 o'clock in the evening and Jennifer came walking out before they reached the house. Looking at Chris, she said, "shall we treat our guest by taking him to a restaurant tonight?"

"Yes, sounds like a great idea," said Chris, "I know just the place - the Italian restaurant with the great food. Like Italian food, Nick?"

"Grew up on it, liked the spicy type."

"It's a really great place, quiet and good food," said Jennifer.

"Let's do it, will be interesting to see what the restaurants are like," said Nick as he laughed.

They all laughed, went inside the house to get ready. Twenty minutes later they got into the SUV and drove to the restaurant. Nick was amused that everything was so 'manual', no menu screens, no estimating the food arrival time, but he enjoyed it.

"You know, this is a more personal setting with everything done by people, rather than with displays - something is lost the way we do it in twenty one '0' four."

During dinner they discussed what they were going to do tomorrow when they got to 2104. What was Nick going to tell his partner?

"We'll have to see what happened to Geoff and Mike, maybe they're in jail," said Jennifer.

"If I explain the situation to my partner she might help us, I don't know for sure but wouldn't want to jeopardize her job."

Changing the subject, Nick continued.

"I need the gun and other equipment before going back, how can we get them?"

"There's a way," said Chris. "We could go to 2104, get the portable time devices, then go back to twenty seventy two and get the gun."

"Why the time devices," said Jennifer, "Chris, you had a problem with yours, are they reliable?"

"They're reliable, we can use them to get into the building, find the gun and get back outside. The problem is, leaving from inside the building, we'll end up in the same place when we return."

"When I got released they took me to the evidence room to get my things, It's actually in the same place as in oh four," said Nick.

"The devices don't work like the TS, there might be a way to do a modification to start outside the building, but materialize inside."

"Chris, if you do the modification it would make it a lot easier to get the gun," said Nick, "what about the pouch and communicator, any way of retrieving them?"

"Do you know the approximate time the pouch came off, I might be able to calculate a time if you knew how many seconds before you let go. That's hard to do I know, but it's a start to find out the time it landed."

Before Nick could answer .... Jennifer spoke up, "I looked at the time indicators - it was January 15 about 1:00 am in 2073."

Chris turned to Jennifer. "I didn't know you saw the time."

"Forgot to mention it in all the confusion, Nick's time was more important."

"If the time is reasonably accurate, we can go back, pick them up just by getting there before 1:00 am and waiting for them to materialize," said Chris.

"Ok, let's try it," said Nick.

"Tomorrow morning we'll go to 2104, get the time traveling devices, retrieve the pouch and communicator then we'll get the gun."

"You two go," said Jennifer.

"Are you sure you don't want to go to twenty one 'O' four?" asked Chris.

"No, that's a short turn around trip."

They finished their meal, got in the SUV and drove home.

They said their 'good nights', Nick went to his room and Jennifer and Chris went upstairs to bed.

The next morning at about 9:15 am, Jennifer was awakened by noises from the kitchen.

"Nick, is that you."

"Yes," came the response, "just trying to make coffee."

"Hold on, I'll be right down."

Just then Chris woke up. "What's going on?"

"Nick is in the kitchen trying to make coffee, I'm going down to help him again."

Jennifer walked down in her robe and slippers. "Let me do that."

"Still not used to making coffee with this type of machine, can you show me again?"

She showed him, making coffee at the same time, but he kept explaining about the coffee machines in the future.

"The machines in 2104 are attached to the water and have a coffee bin, all that's needed is to put a cup on the tray and press a button. You select what you want, water temperature, cream, sugar or sweetener and it comes out ready made."

"Well, we still have to do it by ourselves - those machines haven't been invented yet." She filled the machine with coffee and water then turned it on as Chris was coming down in his robe. "Good morning, everyone sleep well?"

"Great," said Nick. "When do you want to go?"

"In a few hours.............. after I wake up."

"Ok, would sure like to get this over with soon."

They had their coffee and breakfast, got dressed and in a few hours they were ready to go.

Chris and Nick got into the TS. Chris looked at his watch; it was forty-seven minutes past eleven. The date was set for August 6, 2104, 5 pm. He pressed the button, moved the switch and they were on their way to the future. Seemed like only minutes for them to get there, even going through the seasonal and day/night changes.

"I'll be back in a few minutes, will just pick the devices up and be right out," Chris said.

"I'm not going any place," said Nick.

Chris went into the house, down to the basement, removed the loose boards and got the time devices and the suits. He set the boards back in place. At the TS he put the time devices on the back seat, set the time for September 2, 2004 at 12:30 pm, pressed the button, moved the switch and they were on their way back.

Back in 2004, Chris took the time devices and suits out of the TS and put them on the table near the computers.

When Jennifer saw them back in the house, she commented, "Haven't you left yet?"

"Just got back, Jennifer," said Nick.

"That was fast, did you get the time devices?"

"The time devices and the suits too," said Chris.

"We'll leave this afternoon for the pouch and communicator. I want to check the devices, the last time we used them the arrival times were different."

Chris changed the subject.................................

"I've been thinking of a way we can get to the place the pouch and communicator landed. Jennifer, you drive Nick and I to the alley beside the place we left from in twenty one 'O' four, we'll land in twenty seventy three at the same place and watch for the pouch and communicator to materialize."

"We'll set the return time for an hour after we leave and you can pick us up there making it clean and simple. If we land here in seventy three we have to get to the city without transportation – could get questions with us carrying the time device."

"Sounds like a plan," said Nick, "when I landed in seventy two that's the alley I went into."

"Ok" said Jennifer. "I'll drive you there and pick you up in an hour."

In the afternoon Chris did some adjustments on the time devices.

"Everything is working ok, ready to go."

"Let's do it," said Nick.

"Can you get the money we had left from seventy two," he said to Jennifer.

"It's on the table near the computers." she got the money and handed it to Chris.

"Thanks, hope we don't have to use any of this."

Chris got the magnetic umbrellas from the table and as he was handing one to Nick, "where'd you get those umbrellas?"

"Got them in your time, quite the devices."

"This model hasn't been available for too long."

"Were ready," said Chris. "Set the top indicator to January 15, 2073 at 12:50 am."

Chris looked at his wrist watch - the time was 4:17 pm. "Set the bottom indicator for September 2, 2004 at 6 pm."

They grabbed their jackets, got into the regular SUV, drove to the alley and parked just far enough down that they couldn't be seen easily from the main road. There were people walking in the street but no one was in the alley. Chris and Nick got out of the SUV and moved towards the wall of a building just in front of the driver's side. "Stand at least five feet from the SUV," Chris said to Nick, "Don't want the time devices to affect Jennifer." Nick stepped back beside Chris. "You sure these things work?"

"Guaranteed, been used only once before," as he gave a laugh. Jennifer and Nick laughed also.

"Ok, let's do it," said Nick, "got the magnetic umbrellas?"

"Right, here," as Chris handed him one.

"Better stay close to the building, could get hit if something comes down the alley when we materialize."

"Is your top time indicator set for January 15, 2073 at 12:50 am," said Chris.

Nick looked at his indicator. "That's confirmed."

"Ok, we're set, take the umbrella and turn it to full protection."

"The time is 4:52," as he looked at his watch.

"I have about the same, 4:53," said Jennifer.

"The return is set for 6:00 pm," said Chris.

"Ok, I'll be back at that time .... be careful you two."

Both Chris and Nick waved and turned the time travel devices 'ON'. They held the box for the magnetic umbrellas on top of the time device, then turned it "ON" and set the slider control to full protection. There was a 'woo.....sh' sound as the umbrellas encompassed them totally. Jennifer could see them encased by the umbrellas as blurry forms, almost like they were in a clear bubble then disappear. They pressed the 'START T TRIP' button and were on their way to 2073.

The magnetic umbrellas protected them from all the weather conditions. They experienced the changes in the surroundings, night and day passing and the weather conditions but didn't feel any of the rain, hail or snow.

It was dark when Nick arrived, with some light shining dimly from the street on him. A police car was stopped in front of the alley entrance and a police officer was shining a flashlight almost where Nick was standing. When Nick saw this he stepped back, turned the umbrella off and hid behind a garbage bin. A minute later, a few feet from where Nick had landed, Chris arrived. He turned the umbrella off, couldn't see Nick, but saw something that looked like the light from a flashlight on the wall on the other side of the alley. All of a sudden a hand reached out and pulled Chris behind the bin.

"S......sh, it's me, how come it took you longer?"

"They're still not set the same, have to work on them again when we get back - what's going on?"

"Probably looking for someone - hope they move soon. We only got about five minutes," said Nick.

"Recheck your return time indicator for September 2, 2004 at 6 pm," said Chris.

Nick checked, then turned to Chris and said, "Checked – September 2, 2004 at 6 pm."

"If we get separated press the 'Return T Trip' button, leave the unit 'ON', it'll be faster to activate the return."

The police car moved slowly down the street and disappeared behind a building.

Nick went down the alley, looked around the corner of the building and saw the police car stopping. He motioned to Chris to stay down. Nick walked in a crouched position back to Chris where they hid behind the garbage bin.

"Have to stay here until they leave," said Nick.

They waited for a few minutes and Nick walked to the building corner to check again. The police car had stopped a little ways from the place where the pouch and communicator should materialize. On the police radio came a voice saying, "We have a report of a 459 (burglary) attempt at 255 Statewide Street." The dispatcher told them to look around the area for anything suspicious at the crossroad of Statewide and Main.

The driver of the police car responded, "Ten four."

Chris walked in a crouched position over to where Nick was standing.

"Nick, what's goin' on?"

"Looks like they're going to look around – they're putting their hats on."

"What's the time," Nick said.

"My watch is still set at the time we left, it's at 4:37, about 1:10 here."

About five feet behind the police car they could see the pouch and communicator materialize on the road.

"Better make a dash for it," said Nick.

Nick ran out, grabbed them and started back. The car doors opened and the police got out of the car. The one on the passenger side saw Nick running into the alley,

"Stop," he yelled.

The other police officer looked, saw Nick running, then pursued him. Nick got to where Chris was standing. "Quick, press the return button," said Chris.

They both leaned against the building, trying not to be seen and pressed the 'RETURN T TRIP' button. The time travel devices were slow to start. The police caught up to them with their guns drawn.

"What are you doing here?"

"What's that in your hand," the other police officer said. Nick was holding his communicator and pouch.

In a few seconds they faded for the return trip. The police officers shone their flashlights on them until they disappeared.

Chris had the umbrellas in his hand but didn't have time to activate it. Nick's hands were holding on to the communicator and pouch. Traveling home they got battered by some of the weather changes.

Back in 2073, the police moved the flashlight beams around the wall searching to find them. Still having their guns out they walked to the backside of the garbage bin, shone the light there – no success.

"Where'd they go?"

"Don't know, they were here, now their gone."

"Better not mention this to anyone, wouldn't want to file a report on this and even if we did, would anyone believe us?"

It was 6:01 pm and Jennifer had been there for ten minutes. Nick appeared first then Chris thirty second later, both about ten feet from where they left.

"What happened?"

Chris told her they didn't have time to activate the magnetic umbrellas and the close call with the police. "We took a weather beating."

"Did you get the communicator and pouch?"

Nick held them up and said. "Yes, safe and sound, no damage."

They got into the SUV and drove home telling Jennifer all that had happened.

"Wow, that was close," she said just as they pulled up in front of the house. "The trip for the gun could even be more difficult," as she looked at Chris sitting in the front seat.

"Yes, we'll have to plan that one better."

"I need a meal and a good night's sleep," said Nick.

"That goes for me too .... I'd sure like a beer – what about you, Nick."

"Yes, would be great and get out of these clothes."

"Let's barbeque some burgers for dinner."

They pulled into the driveway. It was about 6:45 pm.

"I'll turn the barbeque on, then go and change," said Chris.

"I'll get the burgers ready, and bring the beers," said Jennifer.

"Thanks," they responded.

They changed their clothes and went to the barbeque at the back of the house.

Jennifer got them a beer and for herself a glass of wine. They barbequed, enjoyed the meal, talked and about 10:30 pm they were ready for bed.

"Been a long day," said Chris. "Tomorrow morning we'll have to come up with a good plan to get your gun back."

Getting the gun tomorrow could be a lot more difficult than their encounters today.

CHAPTER 25

September 3, 2004. It was 7:12 am - Nick had been up since 6:30 am. He made coffee and the pleasant odor drifted through the kitchen as the coffee collected in the pot. Getting a cup out of the cupboard, it slipped out of his hand, hit the counter, landed on the floor with a high pitched 'thud' and broke into many pieces. The noise woke Chris and Jennifer.

"Is that you Nick," said Chris.

"Yes, broke a cup, sorry about that."

"It's time to get up anyway."

"I'll clean it up - just made the coffee, should be ready in a few minutes."

Ten minutes later Jennifer and Chris came down to the kitchen in their robes. By this time Nick had cleaned up the mess and put the pieces in the garbage.

They sat at the table and Nick poured the coffee.

"It's not difficult to make coffee with that machine, just need a little practice," he said.

"Once you get used to it there's no problem - what time were you up," asked Jennifer.

"About 6:30, I always get up that early, force of habit I guess."

They finished their first cup of coffee.

"I'm going up to shower; you two plan the trip to 2072."

"Ok," said Chris. "I have a way to get your gun," as he turned to Nick. "When I got the time devices, they were designed different than the TS and can be modified to arrive at a different location."

"What do you mean 'arrive at a different location'?"

"They can be set to arrive at a destination almost five hundred feet away from where you left."

"Sounds like what we need," said Nick. "We can start outside and end up inside the building."

"The evidence room is locked up at five, we could do it any time after that. On the midnight shift there's a reduced staff. We could go to the evidence room, easily break the storage area lock, get the gun and we're out."

"Can you modify the time devices like you described?"

"We'll try it, I'll get working on it after breakfast."

Jennifer called from upstairs, "bathroom's clear."

"Be right up," Chris called to Jennifer.

Upstairs he explained to Jennifer what they were planning to do.

"Are you sure it'll work?"

"It should, we'll be in and out when nobody's in the evidence room."

"I don't like it, why does he want that gun back so bad?"

"Don't know, didn't ask the reason."

Jennifer went to the kitchen. Nick was sitting on a chair drinking coffee.

"That's quite a plan you and Chris have."

"It'll work once Chris gets the time devices modified."

"Why is the gun so important?"

"The gun is the latest prototype for crowd control, if it's lost I'd be discharged from the force and be in big trouble. It has to be turned in after every shift. There's another feature, not only the demobilizing and kill, but a special one that can demobilize a whole group of people in one shot, called D\Control. The concern is the criminals getting it. The D\Control works at a hundred and sixty degrees and one hundred and fifty meters even around corners."

"Sound like a military weapon," said Jennifer, "a hundred and fifty meters, that's almost five hundred feet."

"Yes, it's being tried by police officers all over the country under close control."

"Did your partner have one?"

"No, she has the standard issue, no D\Control."

"And that's why I need it back."

"If they get it working in seventy two, there would be a big impact on the weapon's history."

"Trying to retrieve it still sounds dangerous, you or Chris could get hurt or even killed," said Jennifer.

Chris finished upstairs and walked down to the kitchen.

"Well, guess we're all set except for the time devices. I'll get them modified right after breakfast."

After breakfast Chris and Nick poured another cup of coffee and took it out to the TS building.

Chris went to the file cabinet, got his dad's sketches and notes for the time devices and brought them to the table, unfolded them and began to examine them for the modifications. Nick sat in one of the chairs at the table.

After looking at the sketches ....

"The feature has always been here, if another link is added between these two modules," he pointed to a place on the paper, "a different location can be set."

"All I need is a few parts for the modifications." He went to the parts drawers, got some wire and a slide potentiometer (A device like a volume control). This slider had a scale from 0 to 10.

After three and a half hours and cutting a hole in the top of the time device he mounted the potentiometer, soldered some wires, and had them converted.

"This will work, it even has a better feature and you can steer to the place you want to go."

"What do you mean 'steering'?"

"When getting close to the destination, you adjust the potentiometer, to 'steer' to a landing spot, it's quite sensitive, so you gotta' be careful."

"What could happen if you don't steer properly?"

"You could end up on the wrong floor of the detention center."

"When can we try them out?"

"Soon, I'll explain how the steering system works."

Chris spent a half hour explaining to Nick about the steering system, eventually, after many questions he understood.

"We can go tonight after dark, Jennifer can drive us close to the detention center," said Chris.

"We'll need a flashlight and bolt cutters, to cut the lock. I'll sketch out the inside of the building," said Nick.

Chris gave him a pencil and a notepad.

"Looks like this," as Nick sketched the building and the location of the evidence room in the basement.

"That's directly below the main entrance, if we miscalculate we could be in the lobby," said Chris.

"Yes, but if the steering works ok, then it shouldn't be a problem," said Nick in a positive tone.

"There's a ninety five percent chance it'll work," explained Chris.

"What's the other five percent?"

They could end up in the lobby or some other place in the building. They needed to know the distance from where they would be to the building. Chris would bring the night monocular so they could get the distance.

At 9:50 pm they got into the SUV with Jennifer and drove to a clearing just across from the detention center. Chris got the time traveling devices. They put them on, adjusted the straps, fastened them in the front and turned them 'ON'.

"The time is 10:27 pm, set the return time to September 3, 2004 at 11:30 pm. An hour should be ok, in case the timing is off, we don't want to be in the same place at the same time," said Chris.

"Right," as Nick adjusted the thumb wheels accordingly, "all set, return September 3, 2004 at 11:30 pm and I don't want to go through the 'same space' experience again."

"Set the arrival time for May 22, 2072 at 10 pm."

"Right," as Nick adjusted the top indicator, "all set, arrival of May 22, 2072 at 10 pm."

Chris looked at the building through the monocular, the distance was three hundred and twenty two feet, nine inches to the front door. He took a small flashlight out of his pocket and looked at Nick's sketch.

"Your sketch shows the evidence room directly below the lobby," said Chris.

"About how far into the building is it from the entrance door?"

Nick pointed to the sketch where it was, about ten feet into the building. Chris added that and came up with three hundred and thirty two feet, nine inches plus or minus a few inches.

"The slider control allows for up to four hundred and seventy feet, that's slightly more than seventy percent. Set it just above the seven mark, remember, once you start reaching the destination, you'll have to do the fine-tuning. You have only one chance, the timing is very short so if you miss it you could be any place in there," said Chris.

Jennifer was listening to what they were saying, "Are you sure it's going to work?"

"Well, we'll find out shortly, don't worry, the worst we have to do is press the return button and we're out of there as fast as we got in."

"Ok, all set, you take the bolt cutters," said Chris. "Do you have a flashlight and a magnetic umbrella?"

"Yes," as Nick put the flashlight in his pocket, and held the cutters in his left hand."

They walked about ten feet from Jennifer and the SUV. Chris had made a bracket on the time devices for the umbrellas so they didn't have to hold on to them.

"Slide the umbrella into the bracket, turn it on, then to full." Nick turned it on and there was a 'woo.....sh' as a blurry bubble appeared around him.

"How can you walk with those umbrellas blurry," Jennifer said as she stood beside the SUV?

"They're not blurry from the inside, we can see you quite clearly. All set to go Chris."

Chris did the same. There was a 'whoo .... sh' as the magnetic bubble appeared around Chris.

"Ready for the travel on my count," Chris said. "3..., 2.... 1, engage." They both pressed their 'START T TRIP' as Jennifer watched them fade into the future. They went through the usual weather changes, day and night and changing surroundings but where protected by the umbrellas.

When they were close to their destination date they started to 'steer' to the evidence room. Chris adjusted the slider switch and arrived inside the evidence room directly in front of the cage. He turned the umbrella off and it made a soft 'whoo .... sh'. Nick arrived about thirty five seconds later but had some trouble and landed in the hall just outside the evidence room. He turned his umbrella off. He looked to the right, saw a guard at a desk, outside the holding area, sleeping. Hearing the noise the guard stirred slightly, but continued sleeping. Nick tried the door, but it was locked. Chris not seeing Nick looked around and softly called, "Nick, Nick, are you in here?" He heard a light tapping on the door's window. Nick was looking in from the other side with his hands shading his face to see inside. Chris walked to the door, Nick could see Chris when he was close to the window. Chris unlocked the door, opened it and Nick quickly stepped in. Chris then locked it again. The guard heard the door 'click' as it locked, woke up, startled, stood and reached for the door. The guard grabbed the handle but it was locked from the inside. He called the lobby on the intercom for help for a guard to bring a key.

"Quick, cut the lock to the cage," Chris said.

Nick cut the lock and they went inside to look for the box containing the gun.

On the second shelf Chris saw a box. "Nick Brono - Evidence."

"Yes, that's it." Nick reached for the box, opened it and took the gun and holster out.

Meanwhile the guard arrived with a key. Nick heard the lock turn and the door opened. The guards drew their guns, reached in, turned on the lights and came slowly into the room.

Nick quickly set the gun for D\Control, aimed and fired.

A red wave covered the area in front of them and the guards fell down as if they were dead.

"Don't worry, they'll wake up in a few hours with real bad headaches."

Nick strapped the belt with the holster to his waist.

"Let's go out the front to the field, I don't want to use the steering control, it's too tricky," said Nick, "didn't have much luck with it."

They walked out of the room, over the guards, and to the bottom of the stairs.

"Ok, what if there's more guards upstairs?" asked Chris.

"I'll set this to demobilize and it will knock them out for an hour or two."

Nick adjusted the gun and kept it in his hand. They went upstairs. Nick peered around the corner. "There's a guard at the desk, I'll go up to the desk and demobilize him."

Nick went out the door and kept low until he got to the desk. The guard had his back to the main door and was on the intercom trying to find out what was happening. He turned, saw Nick and reached for his gun. Nick pointed his gun at him and fired, "sweet dreams."

A narrow red beam, hit the guard and he fell over in his chair.

"Come on, Chris, all clear."

Nick was looking through the window in the main entrance door when Chris caught up to him.

"Can't see anymore guards, its all clear."

They walked out but down the road they could see cars with lights flashing, coming towards them. Back into the building they went just as the cars pulled up to the parking lot. Two police officers got out of one of the cars, drew their guns and on a speaker one said, "drop your weapons and come out with your hands up."

Nick opened the door and yelled. "OK, we're coming out."

"Toss your weapons out first."

"Ok," replied Nick.

Nick set the gun for D\Control.

"Chris, hold the door about 8 inches open, I'll lie on the floor, when you get it open I'll stick the gun out and fire." Nick laid on the floor, Chris yelled. "Coming out," and opened the door slightly.

When the door was open enough Nick stuck the barrel of the gun out the door and fired.

A red wave spread out and the police fell to the ground.

"That'll keep them quiet for a while."

"You sure like using that gun," said Chris.

"Haven't had the opportunity to use it for real, only on target practice, it sure works great."

They stepped over the police lying on the ground, to the spot they left from in 2004. They turned the magnetic umbrellas 'ON', set the sliders to zero, pressed 'RETURN T TRIP' button and faded to 2004.

Chris arrived first, then Nick about fifteen seconds later. They turned the umbrellas off.

Jennifer was waiting in the SUV. They took off the devices, put them in the back seat, got in and headed for home.

"How did it go?" asked Jennifer.

"That was quite an experience," said Chris.

"A guard called for help then for backup police."

"Sure glad Nick was there, I wouldn't have known what to do."

As they drove home Chris explained to Jennifer all that happened. She said they could have been hurt or killed. Nick expressed that it was exciting. They pulled into the yard. Chris got the devices out of the car, put them in the TS building, and locked the door. He walked to Nick and Jennifer who were waiting for him and they all went into the house together.

"Good night," said Nick.

"Good night," they replied.

Tomorrow they would return Nick to 2104, and bring Geoff and Mike back from the future.

CHAPTER 26

September 4, 2004. It was early morning. Nick wasn't up at his regular time although he was the first up at 7:20 am. He was making coffee when Jennifer heard him in the kitchen. He accidentally hit a cup on the side of the cupboard. She was lying on her right side, opened her eyes, with a few slow blinks, and woke up, looked at the clock and it was 7:52 am. Chris was sleeping on his left side, startled, rolled onto to his back, blinked a few times and slowly opened his eyes.

"What's the time?"

"7:52," replied Jennifer.

"Getting late, better get up"

"Well," said Jennifer, "Nick has his pouch, communicator and gun and probably ready to go back."

"You shower first and I'll just relax in bed," said Chris.

The aroma of the coffee started coming upstairs.

"Nick must have the coffee on," she said walking into the bathroom.

"Yes, and it smells particularly good this morning."

Twenty minutes later Jennifer had showered and came out of the bathroom. Chris got out of bed and went into the bathroom. Jennifer got dressed and went down stairs. Nick was sitting at the table having coffee. Jennifer got a cup, poured the coffee and sat at the table across from Nick.

"I'm ready to go back and get things back to normal," said Nick.

"After we resolve the Geoff and Mike problem, I hope we can get back to a normal routine also. We sure didn't expect things to happen like they did, I mean the TS getting stolen, should've known when we had the break in, they'd be back," said Jennifer.

"The memory problem will be taken care of if I can get my doctor friend Roger, uh...........h, Roger Kempton to do an MM on them," assured Nick.

"That would solve the problem when we bring them back to keep them quiet. What's the success rate for the MM?"

"From what I understand it's about one hundred percent, haven't heard of any that reversed. The way it works, from what I've been told, is on the brain's hippocampus area somehow by permanently erasing some of the memory, similar to erasing an area of a computer memory card, then inserting data again."

"That seems like quite something," said Jennifer.

"It actually has been very helpful for trauma victims, forgetting a terrifying situation, and not having flash backs."

Just then Chris walked into the kitchen.

"That coffee sure smells good this morning. Do we have a plan on how we're going to deal with Geoff and Mike by removing their memory of this little adventure?"

"I was just telling Jennifer that I'll see if I can get Roger, that's the doc who does the MM, to help us. Think he probably will once we explain what happened."

"Where would Geoff and Mike be now?" asked Chris.

"Depending on the time we go back, Kim would take them down to the precinct. They've probably been questioned and if they insist they were from the past they would have a psychiatrist analyze them. With no identity chip in their neck - that would really confuse things.

"If we get back just after we left then all that wouldn't have happened. If they're in the precinct it would be more difficult to get them out. The problem is Kim called for backup and they respond very fast. I think the request she gave was only for two additional officers. We can work something out with her if we get back at the proper time."

"What about the TS disappearing and the crowd," said Chris.

"Don't know, that'll probably get in the papers. Someone like a government agency will probably give an explanation for it though. They don't like strange things happening and not having an explanation. You know what they say about flying saucers."

"Do they still say there are no flying saucers in 2104?" asked Chris.

"Yep, even with the moon base, aliens have been videoed on the moon and leaked to the public, but they still deny it."

"I'll check and see the time we returned from 2104, set the trip with enough time to get there before the time that we left. Uh…………, did you get that???? You know the time we made the return trip from twenty one 'O' four and you fell to seventy two."

"I know what you mean," said Nick.

"I hope this works out because if there's two TSs there at the same time, we'll have to keep everything separated," said Jennifer.

"As long as we don't get them close to each other we'll be ok," said Chris.

"We'll have to allow enough time to drive from home to the city, go to the alley and wait there till the TS leaves, sounds strange doesn't it?"

"I know what you mean," said Jennifer. "Let's have some breakfast."

After breakfast, Chris said, "I'll see if I can find the time we left from the computer."

Chris walked to the TS building and sat at the computer that recorded the travel data."

He typed in "TRIP TIMES" and the screen displayed.

1. TRIP 1 - AUGUST 10, 1971, **** HRS.
2. TRIP 2 - AUGUST 5, 2104, **** HRS.
3. TRIP 3 - MAY 17, 2072, 1000 HRS
4. TRIP 4 - AUGUST 6, 2104, 1700 HRS.

WHICH TRIP DO YOU WANT TO DISPLAY?

Chris typed in 2, then RETURN.

The screen displayed,

<u>TRIP 2:</u>

<u>INITIATED:</u> AUGUST 27, 2004, **** HRS

ARRIVED AT DESTINATION: AUGUST 5, 2104, **** HRS

LEFT DESTINATION: AUGUST 6, 2104, **** HRS

ARRIVED AT HOME DESTINATION:

AUGUST 28, 2004, **** HRS

ENERGY USED TO ARRIVE AT DESTINATION .2 %

ENERGY USED TO RETURN FROM DESTINATION 1.1 %

TRAVEL TIME TO DESTINATION: 5.57 MINUTES

TRAVEL TIME FROM DESTINATION: 19.27 MINUTES

Chris looked at the statistics and thought that the insulator was just about to fail taking that long to come back.

Nick and Jennifer walked in as Chris went back to the menu. “What time did we leave?” asked Jennifer.

He turned around in the chair and replied, “The time monitor wasn’t working. It was about 5:30 I think.”

“I believe that’s right. We should probably leave at least an hour or so before,” she said.

“Jennifer and I were talking and have an idea. You know the alley close to where the incident happened? We go to 2104 and drive into the alley and park. I’ll come out just after the TS disappears and tell Kim to cancel the backup call. We drive Geoff and Mike back here. I’ll phone Roger and get him to come here, do the MM and then you can take Mike and Geoff back to 2004.”

“Are you sure Kim will believe you and help us.”

“I’m pretty sure she will, we’ve always been trusting partners.”

“Ok, Chris and I will bring Geoff and Mike out here, Roger does the memory thing here and we leave after it’s done. It's out of the city, no ones around, should be safer," said Jennifer.

"Ok" said Nick. "That's our plan, when do we leave?"

"Let's leave at 1:00 this afternoon and arrive at 2:00 in the afternoon, that'll give us a plenty of time to get to Statewide and Main," said Chris.

"Should be enough time, wouldn't want anyone seeing us in the alley and in the street at the same time," said Jennifer.

"We won't need to pack anything," said Chris.

"Let's take what we did last time just in case we have to stay over for some reason."

"Ok, but I hope that won't happen."

"I'll go, pack our things and be back in about twenty minutes."

Nick changed to his Police Uniform with the utility pouch, communicator and holstered gun. His shoes now were patrol boots, his nametag, badge and jacket on. He was holding his helmet and the books Chris bought him and walked to the TS building.

Chris was still there and had the back of the TS open. "Everything ok," said Nick.

"Yes, everything looks great, just wanted to do a final check."

He closed the back and looked at Nick.

"You definitely look like a police officer now," said Chris.

"Thanks, it feels good to get back into this uniform."

"You know, I noticed that you don't state the city on your shoulder crests," questioned Chris.

"They removed them about six years ago, wanted us to be able to go to anyplace in the state. If we had the city on our crests there could be confusion if another area needed help. The only thing they wanted on the crests is a code which gives the state, county and the number indicating the city; the only exception is the state troopers which have OR-ST."

"Why did they do that?" Chris asked.

Just then Jennifer walked in as Nick was explaining.

"It was so any part of the state and cities could share the police, depending on the situation."

"What's that about sharing police?"

Chris told her what Nick had said.

"Are all the uniforms the same?"

"Yes," said Nick. "The only exception is the dress uniform which can be the choice of the city as to color and type."

"All set to go," said Chris.

"Ok, let's do it," said Nick.

Jennifer placed the bag on the back seat and got into the back of the TS. Nick jumped into the passenger side and Chris into the driver's side. He put the key in the ignition and turned it on, but didn't start the engine.

He set the travel indicator and the time travel began.

The surrounding area began changing. The trip was very smooth, no shaking or unusual noises.

CHAPTER 27

August 6, 2104. It was afternoon when they left. It seemed like only a few minutes for the time trip. Chris started the TS and drove to the city. The traffic was light, more cars were going out of than into the city. They got to Main Street in about thirty-five minutes.

"It's probably a little early to park in the alley," said Chris.

"Better to be early than late in this case," replied Jennifer. "Let's just go there and wait."

Chris drove to the alley, stopped, kept the TS running and rolled down his window. Ten minutes later the TS drove up. Only the back was visible from the alley. A few seconds later, Geoff and Mike ran up to the TS, they lost sight of them behind the building, but heard the banging and yelling. Kim and Nick stopped at the back of the TS and shouted at Geoff and Mike. Kim walked towards the front of the TS, out of sight for a few minutes and then she came back in sight with Mike. She said something to him and Mike laid on the ground, disappearing from sight. They could see Kim walk over to the other side to help Nick. More people on the streets were stopping to watch, blocking their view of what was happening.

"Nick, Jennifer and I will go over and see what's happening. When we see the TS disappear we'll wave for you to come out."

"Ok," said Nick.

Chris turned the ignition off, took the keys from the switch while Nick stayed in the TS. They walked over to the entrance of the alley and were startled at seeing themselves in the TS. Jennifer, in the TS, glanced into the street at the alley. She saw two familiar people standing there, didn't think much of it, more of a coincident. An odd look came on her face, 'no, that's not us', looking back, they were gone.

Chris went to the other side of the alley, out of sight of Jennifer in the TS. Jennifer walked back to the TS and told Nick it'll be a few minutes, get ready, and she will signal him.

She walked back to Chris and said, "now I remember, when we were in the TS, I looked over and saw somebody that looked like you and I standing here. I didn't think much of it, just two people that looked like us, thought I imagined it. I didn't think of it 'til now."

"Seeing us standing in another place is hard to imagine," said Chris, "but with time travel guess it's possible, Nick had the same experience."

The TS started to fade. Jennifer turned around and waved for Nick to come. Nick got out walked to the alley and began forcing his way through the crowd saying, “please move this is police business.”

The crowd had cheered and gasped as the TS faded.

“Where did it go?”

“What happened?”

“Did it vaporize?”

Someone from the crowd yelled. “It’s a UFO, the time traveling type, I’ve seen them before.”

“Dumb ass,” Nick murmured.

Kim stood there amazed. Nick looked at her with a slight smile on his face, “call in a Code twelve? We don’t need help.”

“What happened, where’s the vehicle, where’d you go?” asked Kim.

“Just call the code twelve and I’ll explain later,” ordered Nick.

“This is Doan, we have a Code twelve, SN (situation normal) – Sierra November.”

She put the communicator back on her shoulder clip and looked at Nick. “Where did that vehicle go?”

“It’s actually a long story, let’s get Geoff and Mike to the cruiser.”

“Ok,” she said, a puzzled look on her face, “how do you know their names?”

“I’ll explain when we get them back to the car.”

By now the crowd was dispersing and Nick in a demanding tone said, “move along, everything is under control.” Kim took Geoff and Mike, still calm, to the police cruiser and put them in the back. She reached through the window and turned on a magnetic field protecting the front from the back. Opening the driver’s side door she got in the cruiser. A few minutes later the crowd had dispersed. Nick came to the cruiser and got in.

“What the hell is going on?” she asked.

“Drive around the corner and pull into the first alley.”

She put the flashers ‘ON’ got into the turning lane, went around the corner and into the alley, turned the flashers off.

“Pull up behind that SUV,” he said as he pointed to the TS.

She drove up to the TS, stopped but left the cruiser running.

“That’s the SUV that was out on the street, how in hell did it get here? Talk to me, tell me what’s going on,” she said in a raised tone.

“I need your help, you know when I disappeared there a few minutes ago? I’ve been actually gone for over a week. ”

“What do you mean, this is confusing.”

“Let me explain and I’ll answer all your questions after.”

Just then a police cruiser pulled up and rolled down the window.

“Did you call in the code three then a twelve? Is everything ok.” the officer asked.

Nick rolled down his window. “Yes, thanks for responding.”

“Ok, if anything changes call us.”

“Thanks,” said Nick. “Will do”

The police drove by the TS slowly looking at it but continued moving out the alley. The streets were busy with traffic, it took a little time for them to get into the street. With the police car gone, Nick began to explain to Kim that the vehicle in front of them was a time traveling machine. When he disappeared he was holding onto it and fell into 2072, and they brought him back.

"What do you mean 'fell'?"

"It's hard to explain, but trust me."

"Everything you've said is hard to believe. Are you on drugs or something?" Kim asked.

"I'm perfectly clean."

He went on to explain that Chris and Jennifer were from 2004. The two in the back are from the same time. They stole the time traveling machine and Chris and Jennifer are here to take them back – they don't belong here. He mentioned the problem of them remembering what happened and was going to ask his doctor friend to do an MM.

"You know that's illegal to do without approval."

"Yes, I don't know how else they could return them."

"Wow, this is a lot to try to believe. What do you want me to do? I can see us writing a report 'arrested time travelers', which would be a ticket for psycho testing."

"We'll create some sort of situation to write up," said Nick. "Hope the news people weren't around."

"I don't think they were. We'll move Geoff and Mike to the SUV and leave the calm ropes on them. They'll drive out to the place where they lived a hundred years ago."

"It's deserted now, we'll go back to the station, it's nearly time to get off shift."

It was 3:37 pm and their shift ended at 4:00 pm. They could fill out the report tomorrow as they had 24 hours to do that. Jennifer and Chris were sitting in the TS wondering what was going on.

"What if she doesn't want to cooperate," said Jennifer.

"If they're taking that long to discuss it, Nick likely has her persuaded."

"Set the time unit for 'travel' in case it doesn't work out," said Jennifer.

"I don't want to press the return button, once the button is pressed all that has to be done is move the switch and the return trip starts."

Just then Nick came up to Jennifer's window and motioned for her to roll it down. He explained the plan was that Geoff and Mike would go with them in the TS and to their old home. Nick, Kim and the doc would come there about 7:00 that evening. Jennifer asked if they were handcuffed. Nick said it wasn't necessary because they have calming ropes on their necks and as long as the ropes are on their necks 'they'll do anything you say'.

"They really don't remember much when they have the ropes on."

"Have you contacted the doctor," said Jennifer.

"Not yet, I'll do that when I get home about 5:00 o'clock."

He handed her his SGPhone, a future cell phone that operates from satellites. He told her he would call when they were leaving – just before seven. If she had to call him, 'just press the 'home' button'.

"Ok," replied Jennifer.

Nick walked to the car. Kim and Nick got Geoff and Mike and brought them to the SUV. The driver's side of the TS was too close to a wall and the back door wouldn't open fully. They brought both of them to the passenger side back door and put them into the back seat, Geoff first then Mike.

"Are you sure they'll stay calm?"

"That's a promise," said Nick.

Jennifer looked at Mike and he gave her a 'lazy smile.' Geoff was sitting on a slant with his head towards the door staring and a smile on his face."

After they got Mike and Geoff settled in the TS, Nick turned to Kim and said. "These are my good friends Chris and Jennifer Manlee, over the past few days we've all been through a lot."

"Nice to meet you," Kim said as she bent down slightly to look into the TS.

"Sorry to involve you in this situation," said Chris.

"See you tonight," she said. "Everything will work out even though it's hard to grasp what Nick has told me."

"I can understand that," said Jennifer. "Sometimes I can't believe all the things we've been through in the last few days not even counting the last few weeks."

"Well so long," she said as they walked back to the police cruiser.

Chris started the TS and Jennifer rolled the window up and they drove to the end of the alley. It was busy on the street but finally an opening appeared in the traffic and they drove out to Main Street. In an hour they were at their home in 2104. Chris turned around in the yard and parked where the roll up door was lying on the ground. It was 5:22 pm, they had a little time to wait for Nick, Kim and the doctor. What if the doctor wouldn't agree to do the MM?

CHAPTER 28

August 6, 2104. About 6:32 pm Nick's cell phone rang. Jennifer pressed 'talk'.

"Hello"

"This is Nick, we have to change the time to 8:00, just need a little more time to get everybody together. The doc is going to bring the MM and a sedative that will make them sleep for the trip back, probably about ten to twelve hours, which should give you plenty of time to put them someplace to wake up."

"Whew, I'm sure glad to hear he's willing to help, should we pay him for the service?"

"Na, I've helped him out a few times, that's how we became friends. By the way I didn't know what you wanted for the memory replacement so I told the doc to bring the one of a two-week vacation in Hawaii. It's actually a wild one spending almost every night in the bar and the closest to your time we could get. There's another one on a Moon vacation but I didn't think you'd want to give them that memory, although it might make people they talk to think their nuts. Looks like everything is coming together, see you at 8:00."

"OK, thanks."

Jennifer turned to Chris and explained everything to him including the Hawaii vacation memory.

"The Hawaii one sounds perfect," said Chris.

In a few more hours everything would be back to normal. They waited, occasionally looking at the back seat and talked about other trips they'd like to take. The clock on the phone was 8:12 pm. Jennifer was concerned that something had gone wrong.

"They're probably on the way," Chris said in a reassuring tone.

"Maybe I should phone, find out if there's a problem."

"Let's wait a few minutes, and then phone."

Jennifer kept looking at the phone every few minutes,

8:14, then at 8:16, again at 8:19, finally at 8:20 she pressed 'Home'.

She could hear the phone ring, almost immediately. After four rings the machine answered.

'This is Nick, I can't come to the phone right now, please leave a message.'

Beep................

"Nick, this is Jennifer where are you?"

She hung up. A few minutes later the phone rang, she pressed the talk button. "Hello."

"Jennifer, this is Nick, we need another half hour, the probes for the dual MM are at the hospital. Roger didn't have them in the car."

"Will he be able to get them without any trouble?"

"Yes, just a signing formality," said Nick.

She pressed the cancel button and the conversation ended.

"Any problem?" asked Chris.

"They have to get something called a dual MM probe; it'll take another half hour."

"Just have to wait, can't do much more."

During this time Geoff and Mike were just sitting there giving an odd smile every so often. Mike in a slurry voice said he was thirsty. They didn't have anything to drink, so she told him water was coming. Mike responded politely and asked them to hurry.

"Those devices make them the politest people," Chris said.

At 8:47 pm a vehicle came down the driveway. The lights were too bright, to see who was in the vehicle. It pulled up in front of the house and they could see it was a car. Three people emerged from the car just as the trunk popped open. From what they could see, it looked like Nick, Kim and another person. Nick turned on his flashlight, waited for Kim and Roger to come around to his side.

They walked towards the TS.

"It's Nick and Kim," Jennifer said relieved, "must be Roger too."

Jennifer opened the door and stepped out, leaving the door open so there would be some light where she was standing. She could see it was Nick and Kim as they walked closer to the TS. Chris got out, closed the door and walked to the passenger side beside Jennifer. Nick turned his flashlight off.

"Sorry we're late, have everything including the dual MM."

Kim said, "hi, Nick's been telling me all that happened and it's still hard to believe what the TS can do, that's quite a toy."

"Thanks, we're hoping to have some time traveling fun with it after we get Mike and Geoff back," said Chris.

Roger got the MM out of the trunk and carried it over to the TS. The MM was in an aluminum case, about the size of a normal brief case and six inches thick.

"I'd like you to meet Jennifer and Chris, this is Roger my doctor friend."

"Nice to meet you," Roger said.

"Nice to meet you, we're sure grateful for your help," Chris responded and shook hands with Roger.

"Let's get this done so you can be on your way."

"How long will it take? How does it work?" asked Jennifer.

"Takes about ten minutes, it works in the declarative hippocampus memory in the brain."

Mike asked for water again.

"Has he been asking for water?" asked Roger.

"Yes, a while ago he did," said Jennifer.

"We've got bottled water in the car," said Nick.

Nick went over to the car, came back with a water bottle, took the cap off and handed it to Mike.

"Thank you," as he put it to his mouth and started drinking.

He kept on drinking until only a quarter of it was left. Geoff calmly asked for a drink. Mike handed the bottle to Geoff and he drank all that was remaining. Geoff handed the empty bottle back. "Thank You."

"They sure are mellow with those ropes on," said Jennifer.

"Those ropes have been great, we've only had them for about seven months, it's easier to make arrests and keep the suspects calm," said Kim.

Roger said he was ready to get started and would save a copy of the memory he extracted for Jennifer. Jennifer, with a surprised look, said 'ok', and wondered what she would do with it. Roger set the case on the passenger seat in the TS and opened it up.

Inside was a display screen, an alphanumeric keypad, and dials, gauges and switches. The gauges measure the completion of erasing and replacing of the memory along with the amount of energy (battery) available. The switches were for turning the unit on and enable the memory erasing and replacing. There were two slots in the case one for cards about the size of a credit card and another that had some small cables. The top slot, took up half the space with two thin, clear cables with each cable having two suction cup type of devices at one end and a rectangular plug at the other. The bottom slot had two memory cards.

He plugged the rectangular ends of the cable into the MM. Gently he swung the cables over the front seat, opened the back door where Mike sat and placed the suction cup above each of Mike's eyes. The probes stuck there without any pressure. He went around the other side, opened the door where Geoff was sitting and did the same. He turned the unit on and the screen lit up and displayed 'MEMORY MINDER MODEL 7511'. He pressed the 'RETURN' key and the screen displayed

'DESCRIPTION OF PROCEDURE AND FILE NUMBER'. He typed 'G AND M MEMORY EXTRACT TEST AND FOR THE FILE NUMBER HE PUT IN 'TEST'. He pressed the 'RETURN' key. The screen displayed 'FOR WHAT PERIOD'. He typed in 'PRESENT TO PREVIOUS TWO WEEKS', then pressed 'RETURN'. He put a blank memory storage card in the slot called 'DOWNLOAD', and the Hawaii vacation in the slot marked 'UPLOAD'.

Jennifer watching over his shoulder asked "Why did you type in 'test'?"

"When I type in 'test' the machine works properly but records it as a test, that way there is no record in the machine of this operation."

The screen then displayed 'INSERT CARD WITH MEMORY REPLACEMENT' in 'UPLOAD.' He inserted the card and the screen displayed 'REMOVE IDENTICAL AMOUNT OF MEMORY AND REPLACE.' He typed in 'YES' then pressed 'RETURN'. He checked all the settings and gauges again and everything was correct.

"Ready to go," and turned the switches 'ON'. Geoff and Mike twitched a bit as the unit started working to extract their memory. They got a blank look on their faces and closed their eyes as their memory was being moved to the storage card.

"Are they alright?" asked Chris.

"Yes, that's just a minor side effect, they'll be ok."

The gauge showed the amount of memory being extracted and in five minutes the screen displayed. 'CHECK UPLOAD SLOT FOR CORRECT CARD AND TURN THE SWITCH LABELED UPLOAD ON TO COMPLETE THE PROCESS.' Roger turned the switch and Mike and Geoff started to smile as though they were living the experience.

"That's sure a change from the down load," Chris observed.

In five minutes the transfer was complete and Mike and Geoff were sitting there with their eyes closed and a smile on their faces.

"They will be like that for about three minutes," said Roger. "I'll give them the sedative now and they'll sleep for about twelve hours."

He pulled a small packet out of his jacket pocket. He opened it and took out a liquid ampoule and slid it into a flat-ended syringe device. He pressed it on Mike's arm, the smile went from Mike's face and in seconds he was asleep. Roger inserted another ampoule into the syringe, and did the same to Geoff. Geoff also stopped smiling and went to sleep.

Roger walked around to the front passenger side. "All done, they'll be out for ten to twelve hours."

Jennifer said, "We can't thank you enough for doing this."

"Anything for Nick's friends," replied Roger.

"How do we know it worked," said Jennifer.

"The MM didn't show any errors, and the expression on their faces on the upload is typical for the Hawaii transfer."

He turned the machine off and removed the probes from Mike and Geoff and gave the download card to Jennifer.

"Thanks," she said, wondering what she was going to do with it, she decided not to ask and just accepted it.

Roger packed the MM machine up and carried it back to the car. After putting it in the trunk, he came back.

Kim got a device from her pocket and removed the calming ropes. She removes Mike's by pressing the 'OPEN 1' button and Geoff's by pressing 'OPEN 2' button. She looked at the rope collars and said the energy was getting low and that they usually last about ten hours.

"Well it looks like we're all done," said Chris.

"Just a minute I have something for you," said Nick.

He went over to the car, got a package from the trunk and gave it to them.

"This is a gift for the both of you, something for the great adventure I've had. Open it when you get home."

"Thank you," said Jennifer as she accepted it and placed it on the back seat next to Mike.

On the main road they noticed a car moving slowly, and then it stopped.

"Could be a patrol car," Nick said.

He looked at Chris and Jennifer. "Better get out of here in case it's the police."

They hurried into the TS and Jennifer said, "We'll come back and visit you."

"I'll hold you to that promise," said Nick as he smiled.

"Stand at least three feet back so you don't come on another time travel with us," said Chris.

Nick commented that one experience like that was enough.

Chris set the return time, pressed the button and moved the switch.

"We'll be home just in time for dinner," he said.

Everyone waved as the TS started to fade away.

The car started to come down the driveway and pulled up to them. An elderly man, rolled down the window.

"I saw a dim light from the road and then the bright blue light. What was that blue light anyway," he said.

"Nothing particular just a spotlight we have, we're police officers checking out this area," Kim said.

"Oh," said the driver. "I'm a neighbor from down the road and was wondering what was going on here, nobody's lived here for many years."

"Were just checking it out, we received a call that there was some activity here."

"Some people lived here about a hundred years ago and disappeared, there's a rumor that they were some sort of time travelers. Sometimes you can see lights here as if there are ghosts, when I saw a light this time I thought I'd come and take a look."

"Everything is fine," said Nick.

"Ok," he drove away.

They walked back to the car and got in with Roger at the wheel. He started the car and drove down the driveway. Kim and Nick looked back into the dark where the TS was – sort off hoping they'd come back.

"Gonna' miss them," said Nick.

"Seemed like good people," said Kim.

Roger agreed with that observation.

Kim turned to Nick. "What are we going to put in the report tomorrow?"

"Don't know, let's get some doughnuts and coffee and talk about it."

"Ok" she said, Roger agreed and they drove off to a café.

CHAPTER 29

September 4, 2004. It was early evening when the TS arrived home and gently floated to a stop inside the TS building. What a relief they thought, everything is almost back to normal. The only thing left was to get Geoff and Mike someplace so they could wake up – in ten to twelve hours.

"Let's get them out to the abandoned orchard up the road," Jennifer said.

"That's the one about eight miles from here?" asked Chris.

"Yes, and you know, they must have come here in a car, I'm sure they didn't walk, so the car has to be out on the road some place."

"I didn't see any car parked on the road when Nick and I drove to the city a few days ago, although I wasn't looking for one either. They could've parked it just off the main road, maybe behind some of the bushes," said Chris.

"What about Mike and Geoff, what if they wake up?"

"They just got the sedative, they'll be out for quite a few hours."

They walked up the driveway, towards the main road. To the left were some bushes that looked large enough to partially hide a small car.

"Look, there's something red behind that bush, could be a car," she said and pointed to an area of bushes just off the main road.

"You're right".

Chris walked over, looked behind the bush, and saw a small red car. Grabbing the door handle, he tried to open it - it was locked. They would have to check Mike and Geoff's pockets for a key. They walked back to the TS and opened the back doors. Mike and Geoff were wearing baggy pants and sweatshirts with no upper pockets so it wasn't going to be tough to check the pockets.

"You check Mike and I'll check Geoff," said Chris.

Jennifer took the gift Nick gave them from the back and set it on the table. She checked Mike's front pockets, and then rolled him towards Geoff to check his back pockets and wallet – they were empty. She pulled Mike back to a sitting position near the back door, closed it and walked over to Chris.

Chris was checking Geoff's left pocket.

"Looks like Geoff has the keys."

He reached into Geoff's pocket and pulled out two sets of keys and some other paper.

"The TS keys are here too and he's got some 2104 money."

Turning to Jennifer he said, "anything in Mike's pockets?"

"No, all he had was a comb and nothing from the future in his wallet."

Chris had some trouble moving Geoff to check his back pockets.

"Were going to have to take Mike out and roll Geoff onto the seat."

Chris went to the back door, opened it, carried Mike out and laid him on the floor face up. Back on the other side again he moved Geoff so he was face down on the seat. Geoff and Mike didn't stir as all this was going on.

Chris checked Geoff's back pockets. He removed the wallet from his right back pocket, checked it, nothing in it to link Geoff to the future. He put the wallet back, then rolled Geoff back to the sitting position and closed the door.

Chris carried Mike back to the seat, sat him in the same spot as before and closed the door. They got into the TS and closed the door. Jennifer started the TS and drove to the end of the driveway and stopped. Chris walked over to the bushes, put the key in the door, turned it and the door unlocked. He cupped his hand around his mouth.

"The key worked, follow me."

"Ok, don't go too fast, I don't want them falling over in the back."

Chris started the car and rolled the window down. He stopped for a car driving on the main road and then continued. He signaled with his hand for Jennifer to follow. She followed Chris eight miles to the abandoned orchard and house. They drove down the road, no one was there. They drove to the back and stopped. Chris took the keys out of the ignition switch, rolled down the other windows and opened all the doors. He walked to the TS and opened the passenger door.

"All we have to do is put them in the car and we're done."

He opened Mike's door and put the keys in Mike's pocket. "That should confuse them, Geoff had the keys."

He took their watches off.

"They won't know the time when they wake up."

He carried Mike to the car, laid him down on the front seat. He moved Mike's legs so they were hanging out the window and closed the front doors. He put their watches in the glove box. Geoff was heavier, they both had to carry him to the back seat of the car and after struggling to get him in the same position as Mike, they closed the remaining doors with Geoff's legs hanging out the back window.

"Whew," Chris said, a little out of breath, "that was tough .... but we're finally done."

Jennifer was out of breath as well. "I hope that memory erasing worked."

"Roger .... was quite confident .... that it was a standard procedure," he said catching his breath between the words.

They got into the TS, sat for a few minutes and smiled at each other. Jennifer reached over, mussed Chris's hair and said, "let's just relax tonight, everything is back to normal." Chris just nodded, and drove home.

CHAPTER 30

September 5, 2004. It was about 4:22 am, still dark out when Geoff started to awaken. He looked at the roof of the car wondering where he was. The only thing he could remember was being on a vacation in Hawaii.

He struggled to get his feet out of the window and into the car. They were sore and cold from being in that position for so long. 'whooo.........o', as he moved them with a painful look on his face. His neck also hurt from being in a cramped position so long. His struggling paid off; eventually he got his feet inside. He reached his hand back of his head for the door handle and opened the door. The interior light came on as he slid out on his back with a 'thump'. He got up slowly, his legs were wobbly and he rubbed his neck. He leaned up against the front door, looked in the front seat where Mike was sleeping.

He leaned in the window and shook Mike's head.

"Mike, Mike get up."

Mike stirred, opened his eyes slowly and stared at the roof.

"Where are we? Oh, my neck is sore, and my feet. Oooo......w" as he tried to move them. Where are we, did we just get back from vacation?"

"I think so, but don't know where we are, get outa' there," he said in a gruff voice.

"Just a minute, till I get my legs outa' the window."

"Come on, get out," as he opened the door and pulled Mike out and stood him up.

Geoff had gained some stability by this time and could stand reasonably steady, but when he let Mike go, his legs still wobbled and he stumbled, putting his hand on the roof of the car.

"Woha...........," he said and they both laughed.

"That was sure a good vacation, I can't remember ever spending so much time in so many bars," said Geoff.

"How'd we get here?" asked Mike.

"Don't know, but it looks familiar, guess we had too many drinks when we got back and couldn't drive all the way home."

They both laughed.

"We better get home, I've got to work tomorrow," said Mike.

"So do I, it's Sunday isn't it?" asked Geoff.

"Don't know, could be Monday for all I know."

"What's the time?" asked Mike.

"Don't know, I don't have my watch, where's yours?"

"Don't know."

Geoff reached into his pocket for his keys but couldn't find them. He looked at the ignition to see if they were there, they weren't so he looked at Mike.

"Got my Keys?"

By that time Mike's legs were better and he stood away from the car.

"Why would I have your keys?"

"Check your pockets," Geoff said in a demanding voice.

"I don't have them," as he put his hands in his pocket and pulled out the keys.

Geoff grabbed the keys from his hand.

"How did you get them?"

"I don't know, maybe you gave them to me."

"Oh ya, why would I do that!"

Geoff went around to the driver's side, got in, and closed the door.

Mike got in the passenger side and closed the door.

Geoff started the car and the clock was flashing 12:00 am. Mike looked at it. "Must be midnight."

"Na, I've never set that clock, it always shows that." Mike had never really paid attention to the clock that it was always showing midnight.

They drove down to the main road and could see the city lights in the distance.

"I know where we're at, we turn right."

Geoff turned onto the main road until he got to the turn off to Mike's place.

They didn't talk at all but when they got to Mike's house Geoff said, "see you later."

Mike got out of the car and responded with an, "Uh..huh."

Geoff drove off home.

Mike quietly went into the house and accidentally hit a chair. The chair fell over and made a noise as it hit the floor.

His mother got up and came to the kitchen. "Who's there?"

"It's only me, Mike."

She said in a soft voice, "Where have you been? Why didn't you call?"

"I've been on a two week vacation in Hawaii with Geoff."

"What the hell do you mean by that, you haven't been gone two weeks?"

"I've been two weeks in Hawaii, we sure had a good time going to the bars every night."

"What have you been smokin'?"

"We smoked some cigars in Hawaii."

"Go to bed and we'll talk about it in the morning it's after 5:00 and you've got to get up in a few hours. By the way, the store phoned and asked why you weren't at work, I said you were sick."

He kept saying. "That was one of the best vacations I've ever had."

Mike went to his room, put his headphones on, laid on the bed and listened to some music. He wasn't tired since he just slept for about ten hours.

When Geoff got home everyone was sleeping. He went to his bedroom, wasn't tired so he turned on the TV but was still thinking of the vacation which made him smile.

Hours earlier, Chris and Jennifer got home. When they arrived Chris opened the rollup door with the remote and drove the TS to its place.

"I wonder what Nick got us?" as she went to the table to open the package.

"It's a coffee maker. What a great gift, it's the one from the future he was telling us about."

She opened the box and took the pot out with all the instructions.

"The warranty is good to 2115, please register when you purchase." Jennifer grinned.

"What a warranty, it's more than a lifetime," she giggled.

"We'll have to try it out in the morning," Chris said.

"Ok, let's get something to eat."

"Good idea, I'm beat," said Chris.

They locked the TS, the TS building and went to the house with their futuristic coffee maker package.

They had a sandwich, talked for a while then went upstairs and lay in bed talking.

"Where do you want to go next?" said Chris.

"Haven't given that much thought, probably the old west or back to twenty one 'O' four for Nick's wedding and some shopping. We never did get to meet his fiancé."

"I'd like to go a few thousand of years into the Far Future, wonder what it would be like?"

"That would be interesting but it's too far. You know we could take Rich and his family on a short trip, maybe a hundred years or so. Donna would probably like to do some shopping in the future and we know Nick there," said Jennifer.

"Let's sleep on it and discuss it tomorrow."

They were happy to be home in their own bed and drifted off to sleep, feeling certain that everything was back to normal and dreaming of places they'd like to visit with THE TIME SURVEYOR.